MW01167523

with a Dope Boy 3

By: A. Jova'n

Synopsis--

Rerelease

"Goodbyes hurt the most when the story was not finished."

At a time where Kiarra should be celebrating the life she created, she was forced to mourn a life that was lost. Deontae's death came as a shock to everyone, and it turned Kiarra's life upside down. When she found out who was the cause of her pain, it started a war in the city that no one was prepared for, especially Church. After the smoke clears around her, can Kiarra put the pieces of her life back together, or will the heartbreak be too much for her to bear?

After living in a nightmare for years, Kodi didn't think she could get away from her abusive situation until she finally broke free. Moving on, she was determined to put herself first and stray away from love until she met Gerald. Gerald showed Kodi how a queen should be treated, and nothing could make her come down from the high she got from being with him; not even her strained relationship with her mother. Can Kodi and her mother hash out their differences? Or does their heart-to-heart prove that sometimes it's better to love a person from a distance?

"Fool me once, your loss, end of story." Lauren has never been the one to give second chances, and after Banks showed that he couldn't be trusted, he found out firsthand just how unforgiving she was. Lauren swore she was done with relationships and the headaches they bring until Adonis came along and refused to stay in the friend zone. Will Lauren be receptive to a new love, or did her past ruin it for the future? Find out in the pages of this highly anticipated finale of *Shorty Fell in Love with a Dope Boy 3*.

Previously from part 2...
Deontae

Kiarra texted me earlier, mad because she had just found out she was pregnant, but I was happy as hell. Kenzie was only six months, and she kept saying how we were going to be spending all our money on diapers. She was acting like she was so upset, but I knew she was just as excited as I was to add another little person to our family.

"What are you smiling so hard for, Blak? I see every tooth in your mouth, man."

"Kiarra just found out she's pregnant again."

"Damn, y'all wasn't playing, was you? Having them back to back. At least they'll be close in age. Are y'all done?"

"Hell naw. When she said I do, it was over from there. I'm tryna have a football team full."

Dr. Pierce whistled and patted me on my shoulder. "You're going to need a raise and a second job, brother. Congratulations, though, you seem really happy... Makes me want to go find a Mrs. and settle down or something."

"Thank you, man. I'm about to get out of here so I can get some rest. I'll see you in the morning."

"All right, I'm heading out right behind you. Don't speed too hard to go make baby number three."

"Baby number two didn't even come out yet."

"Shit, the way y'all having 'em, she'll get double pregnant."

I laughed and dapped him up before I walked out the door. I got on the elevator and texted Ki as I was walking to my truck.

Me: *I'm on my way home, bae. I'm starving.*

Kiarra: *OK, I cooked meatloaf, so you don't have to get anything.*

Me: *OK, love you, Mrs. Blak.*

Kiarra: *Love you, too, baby.*

"That must be Kiarra the way you're smiling." I jumped, hearing the unexpected voice, and he quickly wrapped his arm around my neck. My seatbelt was on, so there wasn't much I could do but try to fight him off.

"Aaarrgghh!!"

He shoved something sharp in my chest, and all the air left my lungs. He twisted it, and blood started squirting all over my steering wheel from the wound. My breathing labored, and I tried to stay as still as I could so I wouldn't move the knife that was in me.

"I told her you'll never have her, and I told you, I meant what I said to her." He opened the back door, got out the car, and left me bleeding all over my front seat. I tried to grab my phone, but it was on the floor, and I was trying not to move too much. I saw the elevator doors open, and Dr. Pierce stepped off. I laid on the horn until he looked my way.

BEEEEEEEEPPPPPPPPPPPPPPPPP! BEEP! BEEP! BEEP!

I was laying on the horn and trying to get his attention. He finally looked my way and smiled.

"Damn, Blak, I thought you would've been gone by now. What's going on? OH, SHIT! I NEED HELP OUT HERE!"

He opened my door and checked my wound, then he grabbed his phone and called inside so he could get assistance.

"I need help in the employee parking garage! We got Dr. Blak outside with a stab wound in his chest. Hurry, and get as many hands as you can! Hold on, Blak, they're coming. What the hell happened, man? Who did this to you?"

"Ch-Church. Call Ki-Kiarra. Call. My. Wife. For. Me." It was hard for me to get my words out, but I wanted to make sure someone called Kiarra so she could get here. I needed to see her and my baby if this was going to be it for me.

"I got you, I got you. Don't try to talk. Relax, they're coming. Hold on for me, Blak. Fuck! Fuck! Hurry up! His pulse is faint."

I was pulled out the front seat and rushed into the operating room. There was a bunch of noise as I saw bright lights shining in my face. The medicine they had given me was taking over, and I closed my eyes.

My thoughts drifted to my daughter, and I couldn't remember if I had kissed her before I left out the house or not. I knew I wasn't making it out of this, and it pissed me off because I wouldn't get to see my daughter grow up, or walk her down the aisle. I knew my wife needed me as much as my kids did, but I knew she was strong and was going to hold down the home front. I told Kiarra I had her forever, and that was what I meant. Even in death.

****

Kiarra

I was getting my meatloaf out of the oven when I heard Kenzie scream like somebody was pinching her.

"What's the matter, mommy's baby? You ready to get out that stupid bouncer?" I picked her up, and she stopped crying and started looking around the condo.

"You looking for Daddy? He's on his way home. Let's get your booty cleaned before he gets here, though." I changed her diaper, and we sat watching TV, waiting for Deontae to get home. My cell phone rang, and I thought it was Deontae calling me because he should've been here by now. It wasn't Deontae, but Kim calling me. I started not to answer because I didn't feel like hearing anybody's drama tonight.

"Hello?" There was a bunch of moving around before she came back on the phone.

"Ki, you need to get down here, now!" She was crying hysterically, and I was starting to panic.

"What's wrong, Kim? Are you OK? What happened?"

"It's Deontae! Somebody stabbed him in the parking garage, hurry! He was bleeding so much, and they told me to call you."

I hung up and stood to go get dressed. My head was spinning, and I felt like I was going to pass out. I laid on the floor and called Lauren.

"Hey, boo. Hello? Ki, what's wrong?"

"S-somebody stabbed Deontae. I can't breathe, Lo. I can't breathe, please come help me."

"Oh my God. I'm on my way, bestie. Stay on the phone."

I sat on the phone for twenty minutes, crying and hyperventilating while Lo was on the phone, trying to calm me down. Lauren came in and got Kenzie dressed for me while I tried to get myself together. I threw on some sweatpants and a hoodie and threw a bunch of wipes and diapers in my purse. While I walked back out to the living room, Lo was standing by the door with Kenzie's car seat.

"It's gon' be OK, boo, just think positive."

We rode to the hospital, and I felt like I was in a really bad dream that I couldn't wake up from. The closer we got to the hospital, the more my stomach started to hurt.

"Where's Deontae? Is he OK?" I ran to the nurses' desk, and I knew I looked crazy with my red eyes and hair all over my head, but I needed answers.

"I-I'll go get someone, just wait right here."

I saw Dr. Pierce, and he looked like he was crying. I ran toward him, and he tried to fix himself.

"Dr. Pierce! Where is he? Is he OK?"

He didn't say anything, but he grabbed me and hugged me tightly. Even though he didn't say anything, it still said so much, and I felt my heart instantly break.

"Noooo, please don't tell me he's gone. Where is he? Let me go see. Don't just give up on him, pleeeaasseeee. Go back in there, Pierce!"

"He died on the table. The knife hit a major artery, and he bled out. We tried everything. I'm so sorry, Kiarra." He had tears running down his face, and he walked off.

I broke down in the middle of the floor and cried my little heart out, not caring who was around and looking at me. What was I supposed to tell our kids? Kenzie was too young so she wouldn't remember him, and the new baby wasn't even here yet. We hadn't even been married a year yet, and I was a widow already.

"Ki, you have to get up. Come on, baby." Lo got on the floor with me and hugged me tightly.

"Where's my baby?"

"Kim has her in the family room. Let's get up so we can call his parents." I broke down crying again because I had to break Mama Roxy and Dave's heart, just like mine was.

"Kiarra, wait." Dr. Pierce stopped me from walking and pulled me to the side.

"He said something when I found him before he told me to call you."

"What did he say?"

"Church. He just kept saying church. Do you know what that means?"

"No... I don't. Thank you, Dr. Pierce."

I stomped to the family room, and Lo was standing by the door, waiting for me.

"I called Gio, he's on the way. What's wrong, Ki?"

"Church did this. I'm going to fucking kill him myself, bestie."

"I got yo" back, baby, just let me know. But, we gotta handle this right now."

I nodded in agreement and went into the room to hug my baby girl. I never wanted my kids to experience the pain of losing their father young like I had.

I heard some commotion, and Banks came rushing into the room we were waiting in. "What happened? Kenzie OK?"

"Yes, she's OK...but...something else happened."

"Something like what? Where Tae at?"

I stood frozen, trying to find the best way to put this. There wasn't a good way to put this at all...but here it goes.

Banks

I didn't know what the hell was going on. I had just gotten a text from Lauren saying to get to the hospital now with Kiarra, but now I was standing here in front of Kiarra, and her eyes were bloodshot red, and her hair was all over the place.

"He's gone, Banks. My husband is gone. He killed him." Kiarra broke down crying, and I caught her before she hit the floor. She was crying in my chest and trying to talk, but I couldn't make out anything she was saying.

"You not making sense right now, sis. Who the fuck got killed? I know you not talking about my bro?"

Kiarra looked me in my eyes, and said, "Church killed Deontae."

I stood, staring at Kiarra, waiting for her to say she was just playing or something. Anything except that my cousin and best friend had been taken away from me, but, from the look in her eyes, I knew she was serious.

"Fuuuuccckkkkk!!!" I walked away and punched the wall repeatedly until I couldn't feel the pain in it anymore.

"Gio, calm down, you fucking your hand up." Lauren grabbed me, and I turned to her and laid my head on her shoulder. I knew she didn't give a fuck about me anymore, but she let me cry like a newborn baby on her shoulder anyway.

"It's OK. You gotta stay strong. Kiarra is going to be a mess, and so are his parents. You gotta be strong and hold this family together." She was rubbing my back and talking lowly into my ear, and I just stayed quiet and embraced the moment.

"Gio? What's going on? Why you crying, baby?"

Aunt Roxy and Uncle Dave walked in, and I felt like shit for what I was about to tell them. Kiarra was crying too hard, so I knew she couldn't do it. I wiped my eyes and walked to them.

"I'm sorry, Tt." I got choked up, and they were both just standing there, waiting for me to finish.

"Tae is gone. He got killed, Unc." Aunt Roxy grabbed her chest and fell back against Uncle Dave, who was trying to hold his own self up.

"What do you mean, Giovanni? Where is my baby? Take me to my baby! Who did this to him? Father God, why-yyyy?!?" She was crying, and Uncle Dave had to lead her to a seat so she wouldn't fall out.

"You know who did this, Gio?"

"I'm so sorry, y'all, it was my ex. This is all my fault."

"It's not your fault, Kiarra. You can't control other people's actions. Don't start beating yourself up." Uncle Dave was trying to console Kiarra and his wife, and I was trying to keep my tears in. Kenzie started whining, so Kiarra wiped her face quickly and grabbed her from the white nurse I had never even noticed before.

"I'll go see if he's ready to be seen yet, and I'll be back."

We all sat back, waiting until she came back and led us

to the room where Deontae's body was. Everyone in the room was speechless. Kenzie was reaching for Tae and crying because Kiarra wouldn't put her down.

Looking at my cousin's body lying there lifeless broke my fucking heart. He was all I had left besides my aunt and uncle. I knew shit would never be the same, but I was going to make sure I was there for little Kenzie and Kiarra.

I walked out the room, and Kiarra pulled me to the side. "Don't do nothing without me, Banks." I smacked my lips and was about to walk away until she grabbed my arm again. "I'm not playing. He took my kids' father away from them, and my husband away from me. I want to be the one to end his life."

She had that killer look in her eye, so I agreed and walked out the hospital. Church was going to feel me soon. I had spared his life before, but I was not doing it again. His time was ticking...

Chapter One
Kiarra

"You need to go get your hand looked at, it could be broken." I stopped Banks from leaving the hospital, and he looked down like he didn't even feel the shit.

"I'm straight, sis."

"Bring yo' ass on." I snatched him by his jacket, and we went to a private exam room. I knew I couldn't do the x-ray, but just by looking at his hand, I could tell it was at least fractured. "Can you open and close it," I asked him.

"Just wrap it up or something. I need to get the fuck out of here."

"Can you at least wait for a doctor to come?" He huffed, but still sat waiting with me.

It took an hour to get Banks looked at, and for them to tell us that his hand was indeed fractured. Once his hand was in a splint, we got ready to leave. Mama Roxy and Dave took Kenzie home with them, then I took that dreaded ride home. Lo said she was going to stay with me, and I was glad I didn't have to be alone tonight. Seeing my dinner still sitting on the table caused me to break down again.

"Aawww, Pumpkin, don't cry. You gon' make me cry, too," Lo said, rubbing my back. I laid my head on her lap and continued to cry. After I got myself together, Lo helped me clean the kitchen back up, and we both laid across the sectional.

This can't be my life. That was all I could think as I replayed tonight's events. How did I go from telling my husband about our baby to getting that dreadful call that he was gone? If this was a dream, I needed to wake up now. But, sadly, when I opened my eyes the next morning, and I was still on the couch, I knew it wasn't a dream. I had so many missed notifications on my phone, I didn't know whose call to return first. I honestly didn't feel like talking, so I sent out a group text, telling everybody I was OK, and put my phone on silent. There was literally nothing anyone could do for me unless they could somehow bring Tae back to me.

"Good morning, boo. How you feeling?" Lo asked, sitting up and stretching.

"It feels like I got kangaroo kicked in my chest," I answered truthfully. "I don't know how to feel knowing I have to bury my husband soon."

"I know, baby, but, you're not alone, and you already know that I got yo' front and back."

Since Lauren didn't have any clothes, she left to go pack a bag, and I was stuck in my feelings again. I was able to get myself cleaned up before my phone blew up again. I saw it was Dave calling this time, so I answered in case something was wrong with Kenzie.

"Hello?"

"Hey, it's me, Dave. I was calling to check on you." I had to laugh at him a little because every time he called, he said who it was... like I didn't have caller ID.

"I'm doing OK. Thanks for thinking of me. How are you and Mama Roxy doing?"

"We're fine, baby girl. I was just calling to let you know, if it's too much for you, we'll handle the arrangements for Tae. I know it's soon, but I can't have my son's body just sitting on that cold table."

"If it's not a problem, that'll be fine with me. I just can't handle that right now. But, if you all need me to do anything, just let me know."

"Sure thing, baby girl." After we made plans for me to stop by tomorrow, we got off the phone, and I went through the pictures on my phone to find the perfect ones for the obituary. Staring at the last picture me and Tae had taken together, I cried like a baby. The next time I saw my love's face, he was going to be in a casket.

***

"May his peace be with you, till we meet again.

May his peace be with you, till we meet again.

Till we reach that distant shore,
and we'll shed a tear no more.

May He give you strength to endure,
till we meet again."

I sat in the front pew, staring at Deontae's body in the casket, crying my eyes out as the choir sang "Till We Meet Again" by Kirk Franklin. I'd been crying for a week straight... that was how long I'd been without my husband. You would think my eyes would've dried up by now.

This pain I felt was indescribable. I felt empty and alone... again. The last time I felt this way was when my father was being lowered into the ground, and I didn't think any pain would compare to that. Boy was I wrong.

It was time to view the body, and it felt like I was wearing cement shoes with how heavy my feet were. My heart broke a little more with every step I took forward. I was the first person to stand up, as Mama Roxy sat in her seat, rocking Kenzie back and forth. She had been having outbursts through the whole service, and it broke my heart to hear the pain in her voice when she stood up to speak about her son.

I reached Tae's casket, and I felt my knees buckle underneath me. "Why, Tae? How am I supposed to do this without you?" I leaned down to give him one last kiss before I turned to run out of the funeral home. I made it to the garbage outside and emptied the contents of my stomach.

"You good, sis?" I turned around to see Banks standing there with his eyes low and red. I knew he had been crying just as much as I had, but was trying to be there for me. I appreciated him for this, but I didn't think anything would fix this pain.

"I'll be OK, thanks," I said, wiping the corners of my mouth. We walked back inside, just as the last row was viewing the body, and I walked to the front to get Kenzie. Seeing her face was the only thing that kept me sane right now.

Banks, Dave, Gerald, and Gerald's two brothers carried Deontae's casket out to the hearse, and I got in the designated limo for the family. The whole ride to the cemetery was a blur, and when the limo stopped, my mom had to tap me to get my attention.

"Chubbz, it's gon' be OK. I'll stay here and help you as long as you need me to, OK?" I nodded my head and opened the door so I could get out.

The cemetery was just as packed as the church was, and I didn't think we knew half the people that were there. Reverend Jackson said a prayer, and everyone put their flowers on top of the casket. Seeing this casket being lowered into the ground with my husband's body in it made everything feel real. I had to come to the realization that he was really gone, and all I had left were the memories.

Chapter Two
Banks

After watching my brother get lowered into the fucking dirt, I needed a few fat blunts to relieve my stress. This nigga Church had been hiding out like a little bitch, but best believe his time was coming. I had never cried this much in my damn life. I felt like a female, but shit... I was motherfucking hurt.

Like clockwork, Nicki's ass was calling me, and I ignored that shit. I didn't know what the fuck I was thinking about when I messed with her again. All this hoe wanted was clout, and I was dumb as hell to fuck over Lo like I had, and now I missed her little ass like crazy.

"Wassup, young blood? You good out here?" Law stepped outside with me, and pulled a cigar out his pocket and lit it.

"Yeah, I'm good, just needed some fresh air." I took a pull off my L and blew the smoke in the opposite direction.

"I feel you. I ain't wanna come to Ki 'bout this, but if you need help pulling a needle out of a haystack, I got you." This was just what the fuck I needed. Law had connections I didn't, and I needed all the hands I could get.

"I think I might take you up on that offer."

"Say no more." He took his phone out his pocket and tapped away before he put it back up. "Shouldn't take long."

We walked back inside Kiarra and Tae's place, and just like that, my high was blown. I couldn't come in here knowing he wasn't here; shit was weird as fuck, and I couldn't handle it.

Lauren was sitting on the couch by herself, so I sat next to her, and surprisingly, I didn't get that look from her, telling me to move around. She looked good as hell with her new little haircut. I see she called herself glowing up on me.

"How are you feeling, Gio," she asked looking over at me.

"I mean, shit, how you think I should feel? I just lost my best friend… my blood. I'm fucked up inside, and I can't wait to catch up with that nigga." I didn't mean to snap, but this shit was a touchy-ass subject, for real.

"Look, I might not care about you like I used to, but I'll always have love for you. You need to be smart when you moving around." I was about to speak, but she put her hand up to stop me. "Ki is gonna want to come, and trust me, you not gon' be able to stop her. I think she's still in shock right now, but by the time Church pokes his head out, she'll be good."

"Yeah, I got it. Can we talk about us now?" She fixed her lip to say something, but her phone got her attention. She smiled at whatever the fuck it was, and I wanted to grab that shit out her hand… but I had to remember we weren't together anymore… because of me.

"No thank you, excuse me." Lauren stood up and walked out the door. I swear she had me fucked up.

I needed a fucking drink, so I went to the kitchen to see what they had. When I walked in, Kiarra was standing against the counter, holding a glass of wine. She wasn't drinking it, just sniffing it, looking crazy as hell.

"You got something else besides that wine?"

"Yeah, it's some Patrón in the freezer," she said and walked over to the island to sit down. I grabbed the bottle out the freezer, got a glass out, and filled my cup to the top. I took a big gulp and sat across from Ki. She was staring down into her hands, and I was trying to find something to say to her.

"I ain't good at this comforting shit, especially when I'm hurting like I am, but Imma tell you, we'll both feel better after we handle that situation." She looked up at me, and I swear her eyes changed a different color.

"It won't take the pain away, but at least I'll be able to breathe a little easier." Something behind me caught her attention, and I turned around to see what she was looking at. My blood boiled seeing Lo walk in with that nigga Adonis. Her ass had moved on quick as fuck, and it seemed like I was not the only one who was on some sneaky shit.

I stood up to go approach them, and Ki grabbed my arm. "Don't act a fool in my house, Banks. If you can't take seeing her with somebody else, YOU shouldn't have fucked up." She walked away and went to greet Adonis. Ki had bossed the fuck up on me and left me sitting here feeling and looking shitty. My phone ringing snapped me out of my thoughts. I pulled it out of my pocket and saw Gerald's name flash across the screen.

"Wassup, G?"

"Man, I'm ready to catch a couple bodies. When we making moves? You already know Rome and Darius

SHORTY FELL IN LOVE WITH A DOPE BOY 3

ready, too." Tae's death had fucked a lot of people up, especially since he was the first one out of us to do something better with his life. My nigga wasn't even in the streets; he had lost his life because a nigga was obsessed with his wife.

"I'll let you know. I got Law helping me find the nigga."

"Fuck that. Meet us at my mom's house, we gotta draw that nigga out." I agreed, and we got off the phone, so I could leave out. I hugged my aunt and uncle and told Kiarra I was gone.

When I got outside, it looked gloomy as hell, and the shit matched my mood completely. The ride over to the Morgan Park neighborhood took me about twenty minutes because these motherfuckers acted like they didn't know how to drive with this little-ass drizzling going on.

I pulled up to Gerald's mom's house on 113th and Green, and I saw he and his brothers sitting outside. I parked and got out to meet them on the porch. These niggas were sitting out here smoking like it was nice as fuck outside.

"Wassup, bro? Sorry for your loss, man. You know Tae was our nigga, man," Rome spoke and passed me a blunt he had just rolled.

"Thanks. So, wassup, G?" I nodded my head and turned to Gerald. I wasn't trying to be cold, but I wasn't trying to have a heart-to-heart with another grown-ass man.

"Come on inside." They all got up, and we walked to the basement. There were all types of semi-automatic and automatic guns laid out on the table, and I had my eyes on an AR-15.

"What type of shit y'all 'bout to do?"

"Like I said on the phone, we gotta draw that nigga out. I know what block they make the most money on, so let's go shake some shit up."

"Fuck it, let's go." I grabbed the AR-15, some extra ammo, and left out behind Gerald. I had a few pistols in my ride, I just wanted to test this bitch out one time.

"How you gon' handle that bitch with one hand?" Gerald asked, pointing to my left hand that was wrapped up. I had fractured it punching the wall at the hospital, but I was good.

"I got this, nigga, come on."

We walked out, and Rome walked around the corner to get the ride. He pulled back up with a black Durango, and we all piled in. I knew Church and Tre were moving shit over East, so we headed that way. The little rain had stopped when we made it to one of their main blocks. We were on 79th and Essex, and it was like a regular day in the hood. Fiends were walking up and down the block, and they all kept going to the same building, so I knew that was where we needed to be. Rome parked a few houses down, and we made sure we had vests on. I got out first and jogged around to the back of the house. These stupid niggas had the fucking door open like it wasn't a fucking trap. I swear I didn't see how these niggas' shit had been running smoothly.

I crept inside the opened door and followed the sound of niggas yelling downstairs. Rome and Darius searched upstairs, and Gerald followed me to the basement, making sure not to make too much noise. I made my way downstairs and saw two niggas playing 2K, and four niggas at a card table. I let my gun rip, and I hit the niggas sitting at the table first.

Ratatatat! Pow! Pow!

This bitch had a nice little kick to it, and I got hard watching those niggas' chests split open from the impact of the bullets. Gerald hit the niggas who were playing the game, and I heard some more shots ring out upstairs. We checked the rest of the basement and met his brothers back on the main floor. They were walking from upstairs, and both were holding a duffle bag. I shook my head, and we left out the door.

"Fuck you looking like that for? I wasn't leaving this shit behind. Fuck they gon' do with it?" Darius laughed, getting in the back seat.

We rode to Rome's dip-off spot and ditched the guns. When we pulled back up to their mom's crib, I told them I was leaving, and I got in my car. Lauren crossed my mind, so I texted her as I rode down Halsted.

Me: We didn't get to finish our talk, Lo.

Lauren: That's because there's nothing for us to talk about. Take care of yourself.

I threw my phone in the passenger seat and headed to Nicki's crib. I needed a release bad as fuck, and since Lauren's ass was playing, I had to settle for my second option.

Chapter Three
Church

"Yo?"

"Boss, somebody hit the brown house; it's red as hell in here." I regretted answering my burner phone as I listened to this nigga tell me how I had gotten robbed. I already knew who had done it, I was just waiting for that phone call

"A'ight I'll hit Tre up. I'm on vacation with my family, but I'll be back soon."

I hung up, and Miranda looked over at me from her seat on the couch. "Everything OK?"

"Yeah, I'm good. I gotta step out on the balcony for a minute."

"That's fine, I'm not going anywhere." I wanted to say something I knew was going to hurt her feelings, but I just nodded my head and stepped out on the balcony. We were in Orlando because Miranda swore MJ wanted to come here for his birthday, but it gave me time to get away and get a plan together before we got back home. We were going to be here for a week, so I had more than enough time to keep my head low. But, my brother was still out there, so I had to fill him in.

"Wassup, bro?" Tre answered on the first ring, and it sounded like he was in traffic.

"I need you to lay low for a lil minute. I did some shit, and I don't want motha fuckas to try to touch you to get to me. Niggas hit the crib on Essex, and I know that ain't gon' be the end of it."

I heard him sigh on the other end of the phone before he said, "You did that shit on the news, man? I knew I recognized ol' boy from seeing him with Banks. You murked her guy, Church? It's that serious?"

"You don't fuckin' get it!"

"Naw, nigga, I get you lost yo' mothafucking mind. Yo' ass inherited that shit from Moms I see. You need to get you some help before I end up burying you. I'll lay low, but hit me before you get back to the city."

I agreed, and we got off the phone. My leg was bouncing under the table, and I was fiending for a hit. Miranda caught me one day, and she had a whole fit about me endangering the kids, so I had been trying to stop. That shit was really my medicine. It was the only thing that made the voice in my head shut the fuck up. When I was nine years old, I was diagnosed with schizoaffective disorder, and they had me taking these damn pills that had my head cloudy as hell. Once I went off on my own and started making money, I stopped taking that shit, and the coke was the only thing that helped me.

"How long are you going to be out here, Marshall?" Miranda stuck her head out, and I stood up out of my seat.

"I'm coming now. I'm ready to lay down, I'm tired as fuck."

"When are we going to try for another baby?"

"I ain't tryna talk about all of that right now. We got time, man."

I was thankful that Miranda had chosen to bite her tongue instead of bitching all night. I really just wanted to sleep.

The next morning, I got up, and Miranda had all this shit planned for us to do, and I just wanted to get back to the city to handle this shit. I knew Ki, and I would never be together again, but at least I knew she wouldn't be with that other nigga, either.

CHAPTER FOUR
Kiarra

"Kiarra Jordyn Blak, get yo' ass up and feed my grandbaby in yo' stomach before I have to force feed you." My mom came busting into my room with a tray, and I turned my back to her.

Whap!

"Ow, mommy! You not supposed to hit a pregnant person." She snatched the cover off me and glared down with her hands on her hips. "OK, I'm getting up. When are you and Vince going back home?" I sassed, sitting up.

"Don't question me. My grandbaby told me to stay as long as I want. Now, you need to get up, eat, and go wash that stankin' ass." And with that being said, she walked out my room and closed the door.

I did a little sniff under my arms, and it was a little ripe, so I got up to take a hot shower and wash my hair. As the water cascaded down my body, I silently prayed for it to wash all my pain away. It had only been about three days since we had buried Tae, and it seemed the more days that passed, the worse I felt. I knew they said time heals all wounds, but I didn't think that was the case for me. I was trying to fight this depression for my babies, but I didn't think I had the strength right now.

The day Deontae died, a piece of me died with him. My heart didn't even beat the same anymore. Once again, I found myself breaking down crying. I sat on the shower floor and cried my eyes out. I'd been crying so much, it burned when my tears fell.

Knock, knock!

"Ki, you OK?" I heard Lauren at the door, but I couldn't answer her as I was hyperventilating to control my tears. The door opened and closed, and I looked out the glass shower door to see Lo sitting on the floor with her back against it. "I know you're hurting, baby, but you can't let it take over. You gotta be strong, Ki. KenKen needs you, and so does little Peabody in your stomach."

I laughed a little and wiped the tears from my face. Standing up, I turned the water off, and Lo held my robe out for me. I took it and wrapped it around my body. When I looked at Lo, her eyes were red just like mine, and she gave me a big hug.

"I'm ready to go handle this shit today. I can't sleep knowing Church is still breathing," I said as I went to my sink to handle my hygiene.

"You know I'm ready whenever you are. If you rockin', baby I'm rollin'."

We walked out to my room, and I quickly got dressed before I grabbed the tray my mom had brought in and went to the dining room. All eyes were on me, and I didn't even know all these people were in here. It was my mom, Vince, Lo's parents, Tae's parents, Adonis, and his brother Aaron. Mama Roxy was holding Kenzie, and she started going crazy when she saw me. Guilt instantly consumed me as I thought about how I'd been basically locked in my room while my mom had her. I sat at the table next to Mama Roxy, and she handed Kenzie over to me. I kissed her little face, and she smiled up at me. Church just didn't know how many lives he had ruined that night. After I had spared his life, his ass had basically spat in my face, so all bets were off now.

Once I scarfed down my food, I fed, changed, and played with my baby until she fell asleep. I laid her in her crib, turned the baby monitor on, and closed the door halfway. It was time to get down to business now.

"Kiarra, we're gonna go. Now, don't hesitate to give us a call if you need anything," Dave spoke and gave me a tight hug.

"I will, I promise. You all be safe, love you." I hugged Mama Roxy, and they left out.

"Ki, step on out on the balcony with me for a second." Uncle Law stopped me before I could sit down, and I followed him out. He pulled a cigar out, lit it, and took a long pull. I covered my nose and turned away from him. I hated the smell of those damn things, especially being pregnant. "How you feeling, baby girl?" His eyes were soft and full of sympathy.

"I'm doing—I can't call it yet, it's still hard."

"I got a location." That perked me up really quickly, and I turned to him with eager eyes. "He just got back in town, and I've had a tail on him since. I'll leave the rest to you. Me and your dad taught y'all well. I'm just gon' say be careful out here. I know you're hurt, but you gotta use your head and not your heart on this, got it?"

"Yes, sir." I nodded and thought of every way I could make Church suffer. Going back inside, I let Lo know what I had planned, and she was all for it.

When the sun started going down, everyone left, except Lo, Adonis, and Aaron. My mom agreed to keep Kenzie until I had everything taken care of. Even though she didn't want me to do anything because of the baby, she knew this was something I had to do myself. It was only right.

"Let me get changed, and I'll be ready, Lo." I stood up from my spot on the couch and went to my room to change. I slipped on some black jeans, a black shirt, and an all-black hoodie. I put my hair in a quick ponytail and slipped my black Timberlands on. The way I felt, Church was going to get an old-fashion ass whooping before I took his life. It wasn't going to be a quick death like I was sure he hoped for. Church was going to feel me.

Me: We moving tonight.

Banks: Say no mo.

I sent a text to Banks once I was dressed, and met Lo at the door. She tried to get Adonis to go home, but he wasn't going for that.

"Y'all on some hot girl shit tonight, and me and Bro coming to make sure everything cool." She reluctantly agreed, and we took the black Suburban Uncle Law had dropped off in front of my building.

It was quiet the entire ride over to the east side as I thought about everything I'd dealt with these last couple of years. If I had kept ignoring Church's ass, none of this would be happening right now. I blamed myself just as much as I blamed Church. I should've just let them handle him last year, and Tae would still be here with me.

I pulled up on 87th and Exchange, and there were a few people scattered around outside. As long as there weren't any kids outside, I didn't care if any of these motherfuckers got hit. The house Church was in was in the middle of the block, so I parked at the corner, and we sat there, watching the scenery. I wanted to see Church's face before we made any moves.

A black Charger pulled up, and Tre got out with Church on the passenger side. My heart was beating fast, and my trigger finger was itching. My phone rang, and I saw it was Banks.

"Yo?"

"This like fuckin' Christmas right now. We in place, waiting for you, sis."

"I'm ready. Lay them down outside first. Quietly."

"Heard you." He hung up, and I turned around to look at Adonis and Aaron.

"Y'all don't have to do this, but I thank you for coming. If you want to leave, you can." With that being said, I got out and popped the trunk. Lo was right behind me as she grabbed the weapons she wanted.

"Damn, this shit sexy as hell, I ain't gon' lie," Adonis said, licking his lips at Lo. As always, Aaron was quiet, but he grabbed two pistols and stood to the side. I grabbed my favorite shotgun and closed the trunk. I stayed crouched until I saw those bodies drop in front of the house before I made my way up the block.

Banks walked up from the other direction, mugging Adonis hard as hell. I nudged him so he could focus, and he walked around the back of the house while I stayed in the front. I heard gunshots, but I stayed in my spot. The front door flew open, and Church came running out like the bitch he was. Before he could even get off the porch, I took the small .380 from my back and shot him in the back of the knee.

Pow!

"Ahh, what the fuck?" He fell, so I took the butt of the shotgun and hit him in his head with it. I smiled when he passed out. *Payback, bitch.*

"Take him to the warehouse and wait until I get there. Don't do nothing without me," I spoke to Banks, looking him in the eyes. I wanted him to know how serious I was.

"A'ight, y'all carry this bitch to the trunk," Banks ordered, and I watched them drag Church's unconscious body off.

"At least I got one of them bitches," Banks seethed, walking off in the direction he had come.

I could only guess he was talking about Tre, but I felt no sympathy. He was just a casualty in this war his brother had started.

SHORTY FELL IN LOVE WITH A DOPE BOY 3

Chapter Five
Church

"You fucking stupid, man! Move on! That's all you had to do was move the fuck on!" Tre picked me up from my crib, and this nigga had been yelling ever since I had gotten in the car.

"I couldn't! It ain't that easy!" I yelled, hitting the dashboard. "I can't fuckin' think without her. I couldn't just let her go."

Tre smacked his lips and continued to drive to the one trap we had left. Banks and his people had hit every fucking spot we had, and we needed to move this one before they found it.

Pulling up to the block, everything looked normal, so we got out and went inside the house. All our product had been moved already, we just had to come transport the money. I didn't trust these niggas to move it without pinching off the top, so Tre and I were stopping by to make sure it went smoothly.

"Look, Church, I ain't tryna preach to you and shit, but you see the shit we gotta do because you couldn't let go of some pussy? Is it worth your life?"

Ratatatatatat!!!

Before I got a chance to answer, I saw my brother's body being riddled with bullets. I had seen and done a lot of shit in my day, but seeing Tre hit the floor had to be the worse. My fucking brother was gone all because of my dumbass.

When I woke up and that nigga Banks was standing over me, I thought I was in fucking hell. I didn't know what this nigga was on, but he just stood there. I wasn't scared of death, and I wanted to get this shit over with, so I had to fuck with him.

"Fuck takin' you so long? You start making music and turned pussy?" I taunted him.

Wham!

He hit me hard as fuck in my mouth, and my knees buckled. If I weren't tied to this damn pole, I probably would've fallen.

"Banks! What did I say?" Kiarra came into view, and I smiled unintentionally. She was still as sexy as the day I had met her, but probably a little thicker, in all the right places, too.

"My bad, sis." They sat there talking like I wasn't tied up in front of them. I peeped Lo taking a seat on the other side of the room, and she shot me a death glare. I had flashbacks of her little ass knocking me out with that damn lamp and started getting an instant headache.

"I'll call you when I'm done," Kiarra said to Banks over her shoulder as she stared at me, and he made his way out the door.

"Ki—ahhh!" She kicked me in the same fucking leg she had shot me in and the pain shot up my back.

"Don't fuckin' call my name. I tried, Church. I tried to let you live—why?" Her voice cracked, and I felt bad for a second. "You not gon' say shit?!" Kiarra yelled, kicking me in that same spot again.

"Ahh, shit! Just get it over with, Ki!" I begged.

"You would like that, wouldn't you?" Kiarra pulled a chair out and sat in front of me. "You will never understand the damage you did to someone until the same thing is done to you. That's why I'm here. I'm not going to make it easy on you, not anymore." The way she was talking had me looking at her in a new light. My baby was just as crazy as I was. "You're left handed, right? Is that the hand you killed my husband with?"

"Ki, can we finally have the talk I've wanted to have?"

"Humor me." She stood up and grabbed a machete out of a black duffle she had sitting by the door.

"I love you, Ki, I swear I do. I'm sorry for everything I did, but I couldn't help what I did. The voices, the voices told me to do it!"

"You wanna know what the voices are telling me?"

She brought the machete up, and I closed my eyes.

Wham!

Thud!

The pain from the blade slicing through my wrist was unbearable, and when I heard my hand hit the floor, I wanted to pass out. I was losing so much blood, I felt my body getting cold. When Kiarra rammed a knife into my neck, I was too weak to even react. Looking up, my eyes met Kiarra's, and all I saw was pain. I couldn't speak if I wanted to, and I wanted to tell Ki once more how much I loved her. Shit was crazy. I took my last breath tied to a pole, staring up into Kiarra's dark eyes.

Chapter Six
Kiarra

"Let's go, sis, we 'bout to light this bitch up."

I heard Banks talking to me, but I was stuck staring down at Church's lifeless body. When I thought about all the pain he had caused me over the years, I lost it. I started stomping Church with my size seven Timberlands, and every time my foot connected with a part of his body, I felt a little bit better. I slipped a few times due to the floor being covered in his blood, but I didn't care about any of that; I was going to stomp his ass a new face. When I brought my foot up again, I was being snatched up and carried away.

"Put me the fuck down!" I screamed, trying to fight whoever was holding me, but they had me in a damn bear hug. When we made it outside, I was finally put on my feet, and I turned around, ready to fight.

"It's over, he's gone," Banks said, looking down at me. I was fighting tears. Not for Church's duck ass, but for Tae. He was gone. I looked back at the warehouse and watched as Banks' people poured gasoline all around it.

"You ready, Ki?" Lauren asked. Banks stared at her, but she acted like he wasn't even standing there.

"Yeah, I'll see you around, Banks." I hugged him and got in the back seat of the truck with Lo. Adonis and Aaron were in the front, and he drove us back to my condo. I told him to park it on the next block for it to be picked up and stripped, and we walked around the corner to my place. Adonis hugged me before going to his car, and Aaron just gave me a head nod. I had gotten to know Adonis over the last few months, and he was cool as hell. He and Lo looked cute together. I knew he could handle her ass, but I knew she wasn't going to make it easy on him.

"Are you gon' be OK, pumpkin? I could come back after I get my car."

"If you want to, I'm not going anywhere," I laughed lightly. Lo hugged me tight, and I did the same. After they pulled off, I went inside, and the second I stepped over the threshold, an eerie feeling washed over me. The condo was quiet, and I wished I had gone to Lo's house or somewhere else but here.

Stripping out of my clothes, I put them into a black garbage bag, along with my boots, and set it at the door. I took a long, hot shower and watched all of Church's blood wash down the drain. I stayed in the shower until the water was cold and I was pruned. I stepped out the tub and just stood in front of the mirror, staring at myself. I still had bags under my eyes, and I had to shake my head at my reflection. After I fixed my ponytail, I threw on some shorts and a tank top and went to the living room to watch TV. Lauren had texted me saying she'd be here soon, so I put on a movie and waited for her to get here.

Lauren showed up with Kodi, and they both had their hands full with grocery bags.

"What the hell is all of this?" I asked, looking through the bags and seeing a bunch of junk food.

"Girls' night, bihh! Turn that sad-ass movie off and turn some music on. I'm not spending my Friday night sad when I could be—"

"Riding Adonis' dick," Kodi said, causing me to erupt in laughter. If looks could kill, Kodi would be laid out in my kitchen right now.

"First of all, don't be talking under my clothes, and I'm not riding nothing." Lauren rolled her eyes and walked to the stove to start the meat for the tacos.

We sat around the island and talked while Lo cooked. Once the chicken and steak were done, we all got in straight fat-ass mode and had our plates stacked.

"Have you made a doctor's appointment yet?" Kodi asked, breaking the silence we were sitting in while we stuffed our face.

"Not yet. Imma call Monday."

"If you need me to come with you, just let me know," she offered.

"Un-un, Kodi, I don't know what you think you doing, but that's my godbaby, too. You better gone," Lo joked.

I didn't know what I would do without my family and friends; they had definitely come through for me and kept my spirits up.

Chapter Seven
Lauren

"What you over there smiling so hard for?" I asked Kodi, who had her face glued to her phone.

"Dang, nosy, Gerald texting me. He wants to know if he can come crash our girls' night."

"Damn, you been gone for all of an hour. Y'all make me sick," I said, holding my hand over my mouth like I was about to throw up. Kodi threw a pillow at me, and I ducked.

"Don't be a hater. He's bored at home."

"Tell him he can come. Let me go make me another plate before he gets here, though," Kiarra said, standing up from her seat on the couch.

"You better tell him to come ALONE, too," Kodi laughed, but I was dead-ass serious. I was not about to sit here with Giovanni's ass. It had been months, and his ass still didn't get that I was *done*. Once he touched that dusty bitch Nicki, he had lost me. I might've been nice and was there for him when Tae died, but that was just me having a big heart.

"He's not coming. I'll just take him some food when I leave." Kodi went to make Gerald's plate, and I stayed in my spot on the couch until Ki came back. She sat next to me, and I noticed she kept staring off into space as she ate.

"You OK?" I asked, getting her attention.

"Yeah, just thinking. It's crazy that I'm a widow at

twenty-seven. Like, am I supposed to just move on with my life now? I can't even see myself with anybody else."

"Awww, I know, boo. It's gon' be hard, but I'm sure Deontae would want you happy and not lonely." I tried to make her feel better, and she just nodded.

"Yeah, maybe you're right."

After Kiarra finished her second plate, she ended up going to bed, and just like that, girls' night was over. Kodi stayed for a while longer before she went home. I planned on spending the night, so I took a nice shower and threw on some pajamas. My phone lit up when I went back to the front, and Adonis' name flashed across the screen.

"House of Beauty, this is cutie," I answered, and heard him smack his lips.

"Why you can't answer yo' phone like a regular person?"

"Because I'm not a regular bitch. How can I help you?"

"Come outside." He hung up, and I stared at the phone.

Adonis: Bring yo' ass on!

Laughing at the text, I got up to throw on my Fenty slides and walked outside. It was the end of April, and the chilly night air smacked me as soon as I stepped out, causing my nipples to harden. Adonis was leaning against his Charger, and I stood in front of him with my arms folded across my chest.

"Why you ain't put a damn shirt on before you came out? Get in the car, you testing me."

I looked down at my cami and shrugged before I got in the passenger seat. "I have a shirt on. I know you didn't come over here to see if I had a shirt on," I said once he got in on his side. He didn't say anything, just started the car and pulled off from the curb. "Where are we going?"

"We just riding, chill." We sat in silence for a while, and Adonis kept looking over at me. "What's going on, man?" he finally asked as we were riding down Lakeshore Drive.

"With what?"

"Why you playing like you don't wanna be my girl? I know you feeling me like I'm feeling you, so what's the problem?"

"I'm not ready to—"

"Fuck all that I'm not ready shit. That's an excuse, bro."

"It's not an excuse! I'm not ready to be in no relationship only for a mothafucka to try to play me again. So, if you can't accept that, then I don't know what to tell you."

"How you gon' take what that sucka nigga did out on me? Since we been kickin' it, have I given you any reason to think I wasn't all for you?"

"Naw, but—"

"Exactly! Stop fighting me, Lo." He cut me off before I could even answer, and I wasn't going to lie, seeing him all mad and shit had my kitty thumping. "You just gon' sit there, smirking and shit?"

"Adonis, calm yo' ass down... I was thinking."

"You had more than enough time to think. You my girl and I don't wanna hear shit else about it," Adonis demanded, turning the volume all the way up on the radio. I shook my head at his petty ass and just sat back in the seat. We pulled back up to Kiarra's condo and he parked in the space he was previously in. Getting out, Adonis opened my car and damn near snatched me out the car.

"Nig—" Before I could snap, I was pushed against the car and Adonis attacked me with his lips. This wasn't the first time we had kissed, but this time definitely felt different.

"Imma call you tomorrow, and don't come out the house with this shit on no mo'," Adonis said, pinching my nipple. I popped his hand and walked into the house. I had an early appointment, so I went to the guest room and laid down. I could still smell the Gucci Guilty cologne Adonis wore, and I went to sleep with a smile on my face. I think I had one more relationship in me, and if it didn't work out, I was playing everything moving. I had been trying to keep the dog in me under wraps, but I slowly felt her poking her head out.

Chapter Eight
Kodi

"Come on, bae, I'm not tryna be late, that's wasted money." Gerald shook me, and I wanted to scream.

"Just let me lay here for ten more minutes, please," I whined. He obviously wasn't trying to hear any of that because he snatched the covers off me and smacked me hard on the ass. I jumped up and gave him the nastiest look I could. "I told you about doing that, Gerald. You left a bruise last time."

"I'm sorry, baby. We gotta go, though." He left out the room, and I rolled out the bed. He had finally moved into my place, and everything was going perfectly. Besides the usual man stuff with him leaving the top off the toothpaste and leaving the toilet seat up, it was easy living with him. *Way* easier than my last living arrangement.

It took me about thirty minutes to get my hygiene handled and get dressed. I chose not to wear any makeup since we were going to be in the studio all day. After I fixed my ponytail, I met Gerald in the living room, and he was smoking.

"You look good, baby." I took the blunt from his hand and hit a few times before handing it back.

"Thank you." After I blew the smoke from my mouth, I gave him a kiss, and we were out the door. The ride to the studio was short, and I was in the booth the second we went inside. I always had to get my recording in either early as hell or late as hell. He wouldn't charge me for the sessions, so I worked around his schedule.

"Can you go back to the second verse? I don't feel it how I'm supposed to," I said, taking my headphones halfway off.

"OK, go hard or go home, baby." I was recording my mixtape, and the song I was currently doing, I had written back when I was with Gates. It was special to me, and I wanted it to be perfect.

Around ten o'clock, Gerald's first appointment came, a rapper named Block. So, I wrapped up what I was doing and let him get to work. While I waited, I decided to text and check on Kiarra. My heart was so heavy for her. When I saw her yesterday, her eyes didn't seem to have any type of life in them, so I was glad we had gotten her to smile. She really needed it.

Ki: Hey, boo, I ain't doing nothing, waiting on my mama to bring Kenzie back.

Me: Aawww, Imma come see y'all tomorrow. I know we gon' be in the studio all night.

Ki: That's cool, just let me know when you on yo' way.

I wanted to ask her how she felt, but I was sure she was tired of people asking her that. I knew how I would feel if my crazy-ass ex had killed my husband. I still couldn't believe Church had done that, but I guess I shouldn't be too shocked since he was friends with Gates, and I had seen firsthand what he could do. My phone beeped, snapping me from my thoughts, and I saw Koryn's name pop up.

Koryn: It's not too late to change your mind about coming to the gathering, Kodi. It'll mean a lot to me.

When I read that, I rolled my eyes. I had already told her months ago I wasn't coming anywhere near Rebecca, willingly.

Me: I'm busy that day.

Koryn: I never even told you what day it was, Kodi!

Me: Next month is pretty busy for me, Koryn. I'm not coming.

I had to let her know that one last time because the next time she asked me, I wasn't being nice.

"Ay, you tryna hop on this hook, bae?" Gerald asked, looking over at me. I had been sitting here, zoned out, and I didn't even think I'd heard the song.

"Did he write it already?"

"Yeah, you just gotta go in and sing and spice it up how you want." Gerald handed me the notepad it was on, and after I read it, I agreed. I had him play the song back a few times so I could get the feel of it, then I got in the booth to record. When I was done, Block paid me, and I went back to my spot on the couch.

"Run that to the bank," Gerald said, tossing me the car keys. I mean, I knew it was five thousand dollars, but I was just going to wait for him. But, I didn't argue, I just got up and told him I'd bring us some food back.

I drove to the *Chase* bank on Monroe and made my deposit. Since I was in the mood for *Chick-fil-A*, that was what I grabbed for us to eat. By the time I made it back to the studio, Block was gone, but Gerald was still sitting at his workstation. I put his frosted lemonade on the table next to him, along with his food, and I went back to the couch to eat. I wouldn't be surprised if my butt had a permanent mold on this couch from how often I sat on it.

"When you tryna go find a car?" Gerald asked, smacking on his chicken sandwich.

"Dang, you tired of me driving your car already? We can go next week, whenever we're free."

"You know it ain't a problem for me, baby, but I know you want your own wheels."

"You right."

By the time we got done eating, Gerald had another client coming, and I decided to go home. He said he was going to take an Uber back to the house, so as soon as I got in, I stripped out of my clothes and laid on the bed. I set the alarm for six so I could be up to cook dinner, and I was asleep in seconds.

Chapter Nine
Miranda

"You've reached the voicemail of 773-849—"

"Ugh!" I screamed, throwing my phone down. I had been calling Church's ass nonstop for two days, and he hadn't answered once.

"When the last time you heard from him?" my mom asked. I had come to her house about thirty minutes ago because I was about to go look for him.

"Tre came and got him Friday, and I haven't seen him since. I called everybody, and no one is answering. He didn't tell me nothing, and I'm starting to get worried." Church had been acting weird, and when I asked him what was wrong, he flipped out on me, and I left it alone. I could only guess it had something to do with Kiarra. That bitch was a pain in my ass, and something had to give asap.

"Have you called around to the jails and hospitals?"

Why my dumb ass didn't think to do that? "No, can you help me? He's usually on the east side, so you call the hospitals, I'll call the jails." After about an hour, I didn't have any luck, and my mom was still on a call.

"OK, thank you," my mom said, hanging up. She looked over at me, and she had an uncomfortable look on her face. "Um, we should get dressed."

"Why, you found him?"

"Well... he matches a description of a John Doe at the morgue." When those words left her mouth, my heart dropped down to my stomach.

"Oh my God, no, don't say that." My hands were over my mouth, and I was holding in tears.

"We don't know anything yet, let's just go check and see." We got the kids together, and my mom drove us to the hospital. We arrived at *Trinity Hospital*, and my mom let the receptionist know what we were there for.

"Mrs. Wilson?" I heard someone call from behind me, and I turned to see a man dressed in a blue suit.

"Yes?"

"Hello, my name is Detective Freeman. I'm going to be taking you downstairs. I don't recommend the kids coming, though."

"I'll wait out here," my mom offered. I thanked her and followed the detective down the hall. My heart was beating out of my chest the closer we got to the morgue. We walked into a room, and the detective led me to a thick, two-way glass. The detective looked over at me and asked if I was ready. I nodded my head yes, and he knocked twice on the glass. The coroner pulled the white sheet back, and I almost passed out.

"Noooo! What happened, who did this?!" I was hysterical after seeing Church's dead body, and the detective had to hold me up. I ran out the tiny room and all the way out to the parking lot. I heard my mom calling behind me, but I needed to go outside so I could breathe.

"Mrs. Wilson, are you saying that body in there is your husband?" I hadn't even noticed the detective had followed me out, and he had a small notepad in his hand.

"Yes, that's him."

"I'm sorry for your loss, ma'am. Do you know who would want to harm your husband?"

"No, I don't. We had just come off vacation for our son's birthday, and I haven't seen him since Friday." I couldn't control my tears, so the detective just gave me his card to talk another time. I went back inside the hospital, and my mom was sitting, waiting for me. "Come on, Ma, we can go." I grabbed MJ, and she held Mia's hand. I put MJ in his seat and made sure he was secure before getting in the passenger seat. A truck pulled up next to us, and when the driver got out, I wanted to get out and beat this bitch's ass. Kiarra looked over at me, and I could've sworn this bitch winked at me. She walked across the street where the doctor offices were, and I swear she was lucky I had my kids in the car.

"What happened? Was it him?" My mom finally asked the question I was sure she was dying to know the answer to.

"Yeah, it was him." My voice cracked, and I broke down as the visual of Church popped into my head. It looked like the side of his face had been melted off, and I knew he was going to have to have a closed casket.

"I'm so sorry, baby. Do you think you and the kids are in danger?" My mom knew all about what Church did for a living, and even though she didn't agree with it, she kept her mouth closed.

"No, I'm sure if somebody wanted us, they would've come to us first."

"But, still, I think you should move. Maybe out of state."

"Why would I move out of state by myself? I

wouldn't have any help with the kids."

"To stay alive! Just listen to me for once, Miranda!" I sat back in my seat and pouted like a kid. If I moved, I had to take care of one thing first... Kiarra. I just knew she had something to do with Church getting killed. She just couldn't let him go, but I was going to get her back, and I knew the perfect person to help me.

Me: I need your help with something. Can you meet me soon?

I sent the text out to the one person who I swore I wouldn't talk to again and waited for him to text back.

Maine: Yeah, I'll see you at my house in thirty.

"Ma, I need you to watch the kids for me for a little while."

"OK, just call and check in so I know you're OK."

When we made it back to my mom's house, I helped her in the house with the kids, then hopped in my car and sped over to Maine's house. We had been messing around for a few years before I finally ended it. He had started talking about robbing Church, and I didn't want anything to do with that. I texted him when I was outside, and he was waiting at the door for me.

"What's going on with you? You been crying?" he asked as soon as he saw my face. I hadn't even bothered to check myself in the mirror before I had gotten here, so I knew I looked a mess.

"Church got killed," I said lowly.

"Yeah, I heard about that shit. I heard Tre got hit, too."

What the fuck?

"This is too much. I think my mom is right, I need to leave. But, I need a favor from you." Maine was sitting on the couch and I straddled his lap. I had my arms wrapped around his neck, and I started grinding on him.

"What you want, man?"

"I need you to take care of somebody for me," I said, tracing the scar on his head with my finger. He looked at me like I was crazy for a minute, and it looked like he was thinking about what to say next.

"Who is it?"

After I gave the run down to Maine about where he could find Kiarra, and what she looked like, I sucked his dick and went about my way. I knew Maine was going to handle that for me, so I wasn't leaving, but I was going to stay in the shadows until I knew everything was over and done with.

Chapter Ten
Kiarra

Seeing that bitch Miranda, I was ready to snatch her out that car and beat her ass, but I didn't want to miss my appointment, so I let her live. I didn't want to see any of the doctors from work because I was tired of people looking at me and feeling sorry. So, I picked a new doctor at Trinity. Once I was checked in, I filled out my new patient paperwork and handed them back to the receptionist. Once I was called back, I had to pee in a cup, then I was led to the exam room. The nurse took my vitals, then gave me a gown to change into. She told me the doctor would be in soon, so I sat on the exam table and waited.

Knock! Knock!

"Good afternoon, Mrs. Blak. I'm Dr. Gibson, how are you feeling?" The doctor walked in, and she went right to the sink to wash her hands.

"I'm doing pretty good."

"That's good. Let me just get you to lay back and we can get started." I laid back, and she let the stirrups out from the side of the bed. She performed a pap smear, and this was the part I hated about these appointments. After she finished the exam, she took her gloves off and helped me up, before washing her hands again.

"OK, you seem to be about ten weeks along. You have to schedule the ultrasound and lab work across the street, and we'll have an exact measurement. But, I'm giving I'll day your due date looks to be November 26th. Here's a prescription for your prenatal pills. Do you have any questions?"

"No, thank you." I took the prescription, and Dr. Gibson left out the room.

I got dressed and left out the doctor's office. I needed to go grab Kenzie from her grandparents. Roxy ended up getting her yesterday from my mom, so I had a nice little drive to Richton Park. It took about thirty minutes to get there with the Monday midday traffic, but, I was happy to see my baby when I walked in their house.

"Hey, y'all. Heyyy, mommy's baby." Kenzie reached for me, and I swooped her up, hugging her tight.

"Hey, Ki baby. I just want to warn you, Kenzie has been having night terrors, but they usually only last about twenty seconds," Mama Roxy informed me.

"OK, thank you. And so you all know, your second grandbaby is due in November." They both smiled wide, and Mama Roxy hugged me first before Dave joined us. "And I wanted to run something by y'all because I might need a little more help. Last year, I started taking classes to get my master's and even though it's online, I'll need a few days for homework, so can we come up with a schedule for Kenzie?"

"Whatever you need, just let us know. It's not a problem for us at all."

"Thank you so much." Dave helped me to the car with Kenzie, and I headed home. I had been working to become a nurse practitioner so that Tae and I could open a family clinic. And even though he was gone, I was still going to continue with our goal and get it open by any means necessary. I was going to make my baby proud.

When I got home, there was a bunch of mail jammed into the box, and I was ready to hunt down that mailman because I had told him to stop balling my freaking mail up. It all seemed to be junk, but one letter in particular caught my eye because it was addressed to Kenzie and me. After I had gotten her settled, I opened the letter, and my mouth hung to the floor. This letter was from a lawyer, and it basically explained that Deontae had a half a million-dollar insurance policy that would be split between Kenzie and me. It was crazy that even in his absence, he still found a way to take care of us. I decided right then that I was taking my half and starting an account for the new baby. I didn't necessarily need it, but I knew the kids would when they got of age. They were set for life.

***

Two weeks later...

"I think I want to move," I blurted out to Lo. We were out finding her an outfit for her birthday party later. Leave it to Lauren to wait until the last minute.

"Why, ain't yo' condo paid for?"

"Yeah, but I keep getting weird feelings being in there, and I swear I think Kenzie feels it, too, because when I get those feelings, she'll start screaming at the top of her lungs." Not to mention the night terrors. I wish I knew what she was dreaming about. It breaks my heart seeing my baby scream and cry in her sleep. All I could do is pray over her and wait until she's done."

"Maybe it's Tae," Lauren said, shrugging her shoulders.

"What?"

"His spirit or something. Maybe he's trying to tell you something."

"I don't know if I believe in ghost talking to me, but that's even more reason to move. Maybe we'll move back to Hyde Park."

"I mean, you gon' do what you want, but I don't think you should move." After Lo spoke her piece, we kept on with the shopping. Once she found what she wanted, I went home to get some rest, and she went to the shop to get her hair done.

When I walked in the house, the same creepy feeling washed over me, and I tried to ignore it, but I couldn't. I sat on the couch, and I was actually Googling 'how to get rid of ghosts'. From what I read, they talked about burning herbs, so I made a mental note to go raid Mama Roxy's garden when I picked Kenzie up Monday. My baby had only been gone for a few hours, but I missed her already.

I ended up falling asleep on the couch, and as always, I saw Deontae. This was why I hated going to sleep most of the time. I hated feeling so close to him, only to wake up and realize it was only a dream. After tossing around for a few hours, I finally gave up and got up to do my hair. I wasn't really in the partying mood, but I wasn't going to miss my best friend's celebration of life. We were all going down to Club Promise, and I couldn't wait to see how everything turned out. The owner's wife is an event planner, so all I had to do was tell her what I wanted, and she said she was going to make it happen.

My hair was in its naturally curly state, and I didn't feel like trying to straighten it, so I put a neat bun on top of my head and tied it down with my scarf. After my hair was done, I hopped in the shower and handled my business.

Staring in the half-fogged mirror, I rubbed my still-flat stomach, and a smile spread across my face as I thought of my baby growing inside of me. He or she had been created with love, and I was going to make sure they knew it.

Lauren texted me at nine o'clock on the dot, threatening me, and I still had thirty minutes to meet her at her house. I didn't want to go overboard with makeup, so I did a light beat and got dressed. I wore a hunter green, off-the-shoulder bandage dress that showed my stomach through the midriff cutout. I didn't even look like I was three months pregnant, and I prayed I didn't blow up.

Once I put on my nude, open toe heels, I grabbed my crossbody purse and left out the house. When I got to Lo's house, the party bus was outside, and everybody was waiting on Lo to come down. I was standing outside with Adonis, Aaron, Kodi, Toni, Monecia and Shay. Everybody had come out to party with Lo, and I was starting to feel better about coming out. I felt guilty for partying when my husband had just died a few weeks ago, but I knew if I didn't come, Lo probably wasn't going to go to her own party, and I didn't want her putting her life on hold for me... again.

When Lo finally came outside, we all got on the bus and headed to the club. Lo was *slaying* baby, and she knew it. She wore a long sleeve, black lace dress that stopped in the middle of her thigh, but since Lo had a lot of ass, it was a bit raised in the back. From the look on Adonis' face, he wasn't happy with what she had on, but I loved it!

We pulled up to the club, and there was a long-ass line of people. The bus stopped at the front door, and we all got out. After giving the bouncer our names, we were let in, and I loved the setup. The VIP section we were in had four tables, and they all had black and gold center-pieces and buckets of ice with two gold bottles of Ace of Spades in each. Of course, I wasn't drinking that, so I had an ice bucket with water on the table I sat at.

"Hey, you're Kiarra, right?" I heard from behind me, and I turned around to face a cute, brown-skinned girl.

"Yeah, that's me."

"I'm Melodee. I can see how you're looking at me," she said, laughing. "I just wanted to introduce myself and let you know, if you or any of your guests need anything, find my husband Dame or me." She pointed to the bar, and there was a cute, light-skinned guy behind the bar, and it looked like he was cursing the bartender out.

"Thank you, everything looks good."

"I'm glad you like it. I'll be out of y'all hair. Enjoy your night, and happy birthday," she said, waving at Lauren, who was too busy filling her cup. Melodee walked out, and I took my seat and watched everyone enjoy themselves. I definitely loved this vibe. Everybody seemed to be paired off, except for me, of course, and I knew it was nothing but the alcohol. I just hoped nobody got pregnant in here from how close they were grinding on each other.

Chapter Eleven
Lauren

Dancin' on that stage and it's all for me

In that lingerie that you wore for me

Girl I love the way that you move on me

Meet me in back by the VIP

The DJ was playing Boosie's song "Private Room" and I had my glass in the air as I grinded on Adonis. His eyes were low, and I knew he was high as hell. He kept biting his lip when he looked down at me, and I was ready to be a little thot. Trying to focus on something else, I took a look around our section, and everybody had a bottle to their lips, except for Kiarra, who looked like she was half asleep, and Aaron, who sat back, smoking.

"You ready to get outta here?" Adonis' lips brushed against my ear, and I had to shake the chill that ran down my spine off.

"Yeah." I went to tap Kiarra, and she jumped up like she wasn't three seconds from snoring.

"Y'all ready to go?" she asked, straightening her dress and standing up.

"Yeah, I saw you over here going to sleep, so I'll get you home." We said bye to the people who were staying and made our way outside. We were waiting for our Uber to pull back up when we heard tires screeching, and a white Impala came speeding down the street.

Skrrrtt! Pop! Pop! Pop!

"Ahh!" I screamed, being pushed down to the ground by Adonis. He laid on top of me, and I scrambled trying to get my gun out of my purse. Ever since that stuff had happened with Church, my daddy told us never to leave the house without protection, but with this nigga sprawled across me, I couldn't do shit. I heard the car pull off and I punched Adonis to get off me. "Move, get the hell off me! Ki, where you at?" Adonis got up, and I jumped up and did a full 360 spin looking for Kiarra.

"I'm over here. I think he got shot. Help me move him." I saw Kiarra ducked behind a truck and Aaron was laid on the ground, holding his stomach.

"Yo, what the fuck?" I heard a voice boom from behind me, and it was a sexy-ass, tall, light-skinned guy with a thick-ass beard. "Mel, get my truck, hurry up." He bent down to help Kiarra, and I held Adonis back, trying to calm him down. A black Range came speeding to the front, and the girl whose name I now knew was Melodee, hopped out the driver's seat. "Help me move him," the guy said to Adonis, and he bent down to help Aaron stand.

"Aarrggh!" Aaron was semi-walking to the truck, and he screamed with every step. I hopped in the back with Adonis, Aaron and Ki, and Melodee got back in the driver's seat.

"Take them to the hospital and come back," he said to Melodee, and she agreed. Kiarra told her to go to her condo instead because it was closer, and she sped like a bat out of hell down the street.

When we got to Ki's condo, I thanked Melodee for

everything, and we all got out. Adonis had to damn near carry Aaron up the stairs, and by the time we made it to the top, Ki had thrown some sweats on with her dress and had her little area set up in the living room. She instructed Adonis to lay Aaron on the pullout bed, and she cut his clothes off and got him an IV started to put him to sleep. Sadly, this wasn't the first time I'd had to watch her in go mode like this, but it was still scary when it was someone you cared about with holes in them.

"What's wrong with him? He needs to be in a hospital! What the fuck, Lo?!" Adonis was freaking out because the machine Aaron was hooked up to started going crazy.

"Shut up and calm down, or you gotta leave!" Kiarra yelled as she pushed some medicine into Aaron's IV. The machines started to beep normally, and I breathed a sigh of relief.

"Lo, I need your help." I ran to the kitchen to wash my hands, then grabbed some gloves and a clothing protector. Kiarra removed two bullets from Aaron and stitched him up. Once he was stable, Kiarra told Adonis to move Aaron to her spare bedroom, and she got him hooked up to the monitor that checked his heart rate and blood pressure.

"Y'all can go home and get some rest. He'll be out for a while, and I'll call you when he wakes up. He'll be fine, don't worry," Kiarra said, looking over at Adonis. After thanking Kiarra a million times, we left Ki's place and took one of her cars home. This was not how I imagined spending my birthday.

"Yo, when I find out who the fuck shot my brother,

I'm fuckin' shit up," Adonis seethed, gripping the hell out of the steering wheel.

"Bae, calm down before we crash. I don't wanna die on my birthday." I rubbed his thigh to try to calm him down, and I guess it worked because he wasn't breathing like a dragon anymore.

"My bad, this shit just crazy. You good, though?" he asked, looking over at me. I reached over and gave him a peck on the cheek.

"I'm good."

We made it to my place, and after a shower, we laid in bed, attempting to go to sleep. I was racking my brain trying to see who in the hell would be shooting at us, and I was sure Adonis was doing the same thing, but I knew we would find out sooner or later.

Chapter Twelve
Kiarra

I didn't know what the hell was going on, but all I knew was, one minute, we were leaving the club, everything was good, Adonis and Lo were talking and laughing, and I was checking my phone in case Mama Roxy or Dave had texted me. The next minute, I heard tires screeching, and everything seemed to move in slow motion after that. A white car rolled up, and a guy hopped out, pointing a gun in my direction. When he let his first shot off, I reached into my purse for my .380, but it was too late. I was pushed down, but I heard the bullet fly past my head, then the sound Aaron made when he got hit the first time. I let off a few shots, but I wasn't sure if I had hit him since I couldn't see. The entire time I worked on Aaron, I fought to keep the guys face in my head. I had never seen him before, but the one thing that stood out was he had a scar on his face that looked like the Nike logo sign.

I didn't want to tell Uncle Law, but I knew I needed to before somebody else did. And, I had to remember to call Melodee and thank her and Dame again. The way they moved, it was like that type of stuff was regular for them.

"Aaarrgghh." The sound of Aaron groaning in the guest bedroom snapped me out of my thoughts, and I went to check on him. He was trying to take the IV out his arm, and I had to grab his hand.

"Hold on, if you want me to take it out, I will, but you gotta relax." I had my hand on top of his, and he squinted at me before he laid back.

"Where Don at?" he got out, and his voice was hoarse.

"I'll call him after I check you out. I gotta go grab something first." I rushed out the room to grab my phone and medical bag out of the living room and made sure I had the pain meds. When I came back in, he was trying to pull himself up in the bed and ended up screaming from the pain. Men just had to be hardheaded. "I told you to relax for a minute."

"Man, excuse my language, but that shit hurt." I handed him some water and two hydrocodone, and he took them. I looked at his wounds, and they all looked good. "How's it looking, doc?"

"You'll be good, just in some pain for a while. You were shot three times; two of them were in and out, but the two in your abdomen, I had to remove. You have a few stitches and staples, except in your abdomen. Right now, it's just lightly wrapped because I wanted the swelling to go down a little, so you have to be careful."

"Man, that shit happened so fast. This why I try to stay out the way out here, man," Aaron said as I rewrapped the bandage on his stomach. The medicine started to kick in after a while, and he dozed back off. I left him to rest and went to the living room to text Lo.

Me: Aaron was up, but he went back to sleep. Everything's looking good.

Lo: OK, we just got up, so we'll be there soon.

I put my phone up and went back to reading the chapter for my Contemporary Pharmacotherapeutic class. This was one class that was available for the summer, and I was happy because it was one less class to worry about in the fall. And after that semester, I would be done with yet another degree and should be just about due to deliver then. That was bittersweet. On one hand, I couldn't wait to have my baby, but Tae wouldn't get the chance to see, and they wouldn't get the chance to bond. I was just glad that my babies would always be surrounded by love, no matter what.

Lauren and Adonis showed up about thirty minutes after I had called, and they sat around waiting for Adonis to wake up. Adonis kept thanking me and tried to offer me money, but I turned it down, mainly because I felt guilty about him being caught in the crossfire.

"How you know how to do all that shit? I thought you were a nurse," Adonis asked me.

"I am, but let's just say I had a lot of practice." I got back to doing my homework, and Adonis went to wait in the room for Aaron to wake up.

Chapter Thirteen
Aaron

"Damn, nigga, I'm glad you up, you were snoring loud as hell." My eyes had been open for all of two seconds, and Adonis was starting with his playing shit.

"Come on, man, it's too soon for the jokes." I winced from the pain in my shoulder when I sat up, and reached for the water that sat on the nightstand next to the bed. Kiarra walked into the room with Lo behind her, and they both smiled when they saw me sitting up.

"Good to see you up, bro, but I knew my sis was gon' take care of you," Lo said, halfway hugging me. Kiarra didn't say anything as she checked my bandages and tapped away on an iPad that was in her hand.

"What's your pain on a scale of one to ten, Aaron?" Kiarra asked, looking up at me. I got lost in her eyes, and I couldn't really form a word. She took a small flashlight and shined it in my face, and that snapped me out of my trance.

"Damn!"

"I'm sorry, you spaced out on me. How are you feeling?" she asked again.

"Hungry as hell," I said, trying to lick my lips, but that shit felt like licking sandpaper.

"I can get you something small to put on your stomach. You should be OK to go home tomorrow if you want, and I'll stitch that wound up for you."

"Thank you. Can I get something to drink?"

"Yeah, I'll be back." Kiarra and Lo left out the room, and Adonis sat in the chair next to the bed.

"You gon sit yo' hardhead ass here, or go home and kill yourself?" he asked, looking over at me.

"I need some clothes and shit, and I gotta wash my ass. I can't lay in this bed for however long I need to be."

"I got you, it's in the closet. I'll leave you to get yourself together. Call me if you need me, bro." He dapped me up and left out the room. I was happy he had closed the door, but the nigga could've helped me get my bag first.

"Ahhh!" I was trying to grab my duffle bag, and it felt like an elephant had stomped me in my stomach.

"You OK?" Kiarra came running into the room and just shook her head when she saw me in the closet. "What are you doing?" she asked with her hands on her hips.

"I need to go wash my ass, ma. I can't sit with this dried blood on me."

"Well, you can't quite take a shower or anything yet with that open wound, but I can give you a bed bath."

"Look, I know you just tryna help, but I can't just take a hoe bath and be comfortable." She stared at me with her hands still on her hips for a minute before she walked out, rolling her eyes. When she came back in, she had that same small bag she had earlier.

"Lay back, I'll stitch you up, and you can take a quick shower. By the time you're done, your food should be done so you can come out, or I'll bring it to you, doesn't matter." Her soft voice made the whole situation a lot better than what it was. She used something to numb me, then got started stitching me up. Once she was done, she wrapped it with some kind of waterproof wrap and left back out the room. It was a struggle getting myself in the shower, and I wished I had taken Kiarra up on her offer to do it for me.

After throwing on some boxers and basketball shorts, I limped out the room, breathing like I had just run around the track by the time I made it to the dining room. Kiarra was deep into some books in front of her, and she pushed a nasty looking smoothie in front of me.

"What is this?" I asked, looking for the rest of the food.

"A smoothie. It has kale, blackberries, blueberries and a couple dried prunes. I've been reading up on ways to heal the body naturally, and you need vitamin K."

"I need some chicken or something. This not gon' be enough," I said, taking a look around her kitchen.

"If this does good on your stomach, then we can move on to something solid. You should be moving around better in a couple days, and you'll be fine to go home and take care of yourself."

"Thank you for this. I probably would've died or something if you weren't there."

"Don't thank me just yet. All this probably happened because of me. You were just standing by the wrong girl. Well, everything is open for you if you need it, just please don't bust any stitches or bleed on my couch." Kiarra gathered her books and walked off to her room.

I sat at the table and drunk the smoothie that was supposed to be my dinner. I had to be out for a while, because the last time I woke up, the sun was shining, but now it was pitch black outside. After I drunk the smoothie, which didn't taste bad, I washed my cup out and grabbed a bottle of water out the fridge before going back to the room I was occupying. When I sat on the bed, I noticed there was a bottle of ibuprofen that was prescribed to me sitting on the nightstand, and the sheets on the bed had been changed. I didn't know if she was a ninja or if she had done this when I was in the shower and I had just now noticed. Either way, I was grateful because it was better than being at any hospital.

Getting comfortable in the bed, I grabbed my phone and the remote to the TV to turn it on. I had a couple texts from people checking on me, so I returned them before putting my phone back up. I popped two of the ibuprofens and killed my bottle of water I had brought. After watching SportsCenter for all of ten minutes, I was fighting my sleep, so I turned everything off and drifted off to sleep. This bed was comfortable as hell, but I was ready to get back in my own.

Chapter Fourteen
Kiarra

"Ki, baby, wake up." My eyes popped open, and my heart beat wildly as I looked around the dark room. I knew I had heard Deontae's voice. I'm going crazy.

"I'm sorry for leaving you, baby girl. You know how much I love you and my babies, and I wish I could be there for all of you." I tried to get out the bed, but my legs felt like someone was sitting on them.

"Stop! Please, stop, let me wake up!" I screamed, crying. I couldn't go through this same dream again. I was going to go crazy.

"You have to calm down. Don't stress the baby." Just as I heard his voice again, I smelled his scent, and I felt his presence.

"Tae, I miss you so much. This is so hard without you. Kenzie looks for you, and she cries so hard when she can't find you. What am I supposed to do?" I had been holding up this strong act in front of everybody, but I felt like I was going to break at any moment.

"Just know I'm always in your heart and in Kenzie's. You're a strong woman, so I know you will handle everything you have to, but I want you to move on. You don't have to feel guilty if you find someone tomorrow or years from now. Be happy." I felt a chill go down my body, then I didn't feel... anything. Just like that, he was gone again, and I cried so hard, my body shook.

Diiinnnnggg!

The sound of my alarm going off made me jump up, and my nightgown stuck to my body from all the sweat. I still had fresh tears on my face, and I had to get on my knees to say a quick prayer before I got up to continue my morning routine. This was the third night in a row that I'd had that dream, and I always woke up, drenched in sweat. I couldn't remember the last time I had a full night's rest, and it was driving me crazy.

"Good morning," Aaron said from behind me, scaring the shit out of me. I honestly had forgotten he was here.

"Shit, you can't sneak up on people like that," I said with my hand over my heart. It felt like my heart was beating out of my chest.

"My fault, I didn't mean to scare you. I just wanted to let you know that I was gon' be gettin' out of yo' hair today, and I appreciate you for making sure I was straight these last couple of days."

"You don't have to thank me. Like I said before, I'm sure those bullets were meant for me anyway." I laughed it off and continued to cook. I made us both a spinach, ham and cheese omelet, and we ate in silence. Adonis came to get Aaron shortly after we finished eating, so I checked his bandages and gave him care instructions before he left. I was happy that Kenzie was coming back home today because I hated being home alone now.

After I got the kitchen cleaned, I called Banks to check on him since I hadn't really talked to him since last week.

"Wassup, sis, you good?" He answered on the second ring, and I could hear him moving around.

"Yeah, I just needed to know if you know anything about a brown-skinned guy with a scar on his face that looks like a Nike logo?"

"Uuuhhh... not that I can think of off the top of my head, why?" I let him know what had happened outside the club and he went off before telling me he'd call me back. Banks was really like a brother to me, and I hated that he couldn't treat Lo right. I loved them together.

Twenty minutes later, I received a text from Banks saying he was handling my problem and not to worry, so I wasn't going to worry about it.

Chapter Fifteen
Banks

Shit had been hard since Tae had been gone, but I just threw myself into my music. When Kiarra called, I was in the studio, but I ended that quick when she told me some nigga had shot at her. Man, it was like the minute I got comfortable, that was when shit started hitting the fan. But, I had made a promise that I was going to make sure Ki and Kenzie were good, so that was what I was going to do. After talking to a few of my guys, they said the guy Ki described sounded like this nigga, Maine. Maine was a known jack boy, and he had so many niggas at his neck, I was surprised he was still breathing. I knew he used to work for Church and Tre's punk ass, so I figured that was why he was gunning for her. After I found out where he laid his head, I hit my guys Rome and Darius up to see if they wanted to ride.

"Yo?" Rome answered, sounding like his ass was running a marathon.

"You tryna get yo' hands dirty?"

"Only way I like 'em. Send me yo' location." We got off the phone, and I told him where to meet me. It was a little past eight o'clock in the evening, and Maine's block was dark as hell, which was perfect for what I was about to do. Rome and Darius slid in my car, and I gave them the rundown on what had happened.

"This bitch-ass nigga, let's go," Darius seethed. We all got out at the same time and made our way to Maine's house. Instead of going around back and doing all that extra shit, I kicked the front door open, and that bitch damn near flew off the hinges.

"What the fuck?!" Maine was sitting on the couch and didn't have time to react before I sent a shot through his shoulder. "Aaahh, shit!" He screamed like a bitch, and that shit was getting on my fucking nerves.

"Shut yo' hoe ass up, nigga," I said, hitting him in the head with the butt of my gun.

"Yo, Banks, what's going on, man? We ain't never had no problems, G." He was on the floor, shaking and stuttering like the pussy he was, and it was pretty comical.

"You right, but when you decided to take some shots at my sis, you fucked up."

"M-man, I was just doing what I was paid to do."

"Who the fuck paid you?" Rome took the words from my mouth, and Maine started singing like a canary.

"This bitch I fuck around with, Miranda. I ain't ask no questions, but she gave me $5,000 and a picture. If I had known that was yo' fam, I would've told her hell naw."

"Yeah, well, you didn't. Yo' fault."

Pew! Pew!

I sent two bullets through the middle of his forehead and walked back out the same way I had come. Darius and Rome came out carrying a couple duffle bags, and I gave them a head nod after they pulled off in their car.

I was going to call Ki, but I knew she was probably, so I was going to get up with her tomorrow. Instead, I just went back to the studio to finish recording. Kodi and I were doing another track together, and she was in the booth, doing the hook. The shit sounded good as fuck, but it had me thinking about Lo. I was pissed at myself for fucking that up, and to be honest, the shit wasn't worth it at all. I had been thinking like a little nigga, and it had cost me my girl. When it was my turn to get in the booth, I poured my heart out in the song, and when I walked out, I felt better about shit. I needed to have a conversation with Lo, for real. I knew we weren't getting back together, but I wanted us to at least be cool.

***

Lauren agreed to meet me after I begged her for like a week straight. Now, I was sitting outside of *Ja' Grill Hyde Park*, waiting for her to show up.

"Did you order yet?" I heard Lo ask from behind me. She sat in the seat across from me and put her purse in the empty chair next to her.

"Damn, that's how you speak? And, naw, I ain't order yet."

"My bad, how you doing, Gio?"

"I'm good, how you been?" The waiter came, interrupting us, so we placed our order and waited for the waiter to leave.

"I've been good," she said, finally answering my question.

"Look, I ain't finna beat around the bush. I know we ain't getting back together, but I still want us to be cool."

"I been over being mad, it's not worth my peace.

You did what you did, and our relationship is over, but if you ever want to talk or whatever, IF it's at a reasonable time, you can call me."

"I respect that. So, is yo' man cool about you being here?"

"Don't worry about my man, BUT, he does know, and he's not worried because unlike you, he knows he got a real one," she said, popping her lips and taking a sip of her drink. I couldn't say shit else after that, so I just sat back and waited for my jerk catfish dinner. The rest of the little lunch went cool, then she said she had to go for an appointment she had at her studio. I paid for our food and walked her to the car. I didn't know if we were going to actually keep in touch, but at least I knew I could call if I wanted.

Chapter Sixteen
Lauren

After I left from lunch with Gio, I had to rush to the studio before I was late for my one o'clock appointment. When I pulled up, I saw Adonis' car, so I stopped in his shop before I went upstairs.

"Wassup, sis?" Aaron said, standing up from the front desk and hugging me. His ass came back, trying to take clients, but Adonis had shut all that down. Now, he was the temporary receptionist.

"Wassup, bro? Your brother in there with somebody?"

"Naw, he just finished up."

"OK, thank you." I walked to the back and found Adonis wiping the tattoo chair down. "Hey, sexy," I said, slapping his butt. He turned around so fast, I thought he was going to knock my head off.

"Lo, stop doing that stupid shit! I thought you were supposed to be upstairs."

"Damn, I can't be down here in this stankin'-ass shop now?" He playfully pushed me and took my leftovers out my hand.

"My bad, baby, how you doing?" he asked, opening the lip and nodding his head.

"I'm good. How long you gon' be here tonight?"

"Shiiiiit, I don't know, probably until like nine at the latest," he shrugged.

"Aw, OK, I might stay at Ki's house tonight. She said

she had an exam to do, so Imma kick it with KenKen."

"A'ight, just stop by before you leave." He kissed me on my lips, and I left out so I could go get set up. I was doing some girl's sweet sixteen photo shoot, and I knew it was probably going to be two hours tops.

After I wrapped up the shoot, I said bye to Adonis and went straight to Ki's house. I let myself in using the key she had given me, and I heard Kenzie talking her butt off in baby talk.

"Heyyy, Gbaby, what you in here talking about?" I picked her up out of her high chair and sat on the stool at the island.

"She about to get a whooping for yelling at me," Kiarra said, turning around from the stove.

"You bet' not touch my baby," I said, kissing Kenzie's cheek. "What you cooking?"

"Some chili. I've been craving it and I just couldn't let it go." I shook my head at her and kept playing with Kenzie. Once Ki was done cooking, she ate and did homework and exams all night. After I had Kenzie bathed and in her own bed, I laid on the couch, watching TV until I fell asleep.

"Noooo!!" I jumped up from the couch when I heard Ki screaming and ran to her room.

"Ki?!" I yelled, bursting into her room and cutting on her light. Her eyes popped open, and she sat up in the bed, looking at me like I was crazy.

"What's wrong, Lo? Kenzie OK?"

"Shit, I was coming to find out the same thing. You were in here screaming. I thought I had to come beat some ass or something."

She sighed heavily, and her shoulders dropped. "I had another dream about Tae. It's been a month, why does this keep happening?" Ki buried her face in her hands, and I got in the bed with her, pulling her into a hug.

"It's gon' be OK, baby, don't cry." I felt so bad for my best friend, and what made it worse, I didn't know what to do to help her. There was really nothing I could do except let her grieve. I hadn't experienced that kind of pain so I couldn't tell her how to feel or what she should do. All I could do was try to make her feel better right now.

"What time is it?" Kiarra asked, wiping her eyes. I looked over at her clock, and that shit said 4:29.

"It's four in the morning."

"Damn, well, I'm about to do some homework. You can sleep in here if you want," she said, scooting over and grabbing the book off her nightstand. Shit, she didn't have to tell me twice.

"Goodnight, boo," I said as I drifted off to sleep.

I didn't wake up until about noon, and I felt like a brand-new person. Kenzie had worn my ass out yesterday. I was glad I didn't have to do this every day or I would look like a zombie. I got out the bed and went to Ki's bathroom to handle my morning business. Once I was done, I went to get my bag out the front and to find out if Ki had cooked or not. That was another reason I loved coming over here: she always fed me.

"Damn, you were tired, huh? I done finished a whole two weeks' worth of homework and you ain't move."

"Shut up, yo' baby drained me. I had to get my energy back on one hundred percent."

"Don't try to blame my sweet baby," Ki laughed. "Your waffles in the microwave." I didn't hear anything else as I took off to the kitchen and warmed my food up. Ki sat at the table with me, and she had her lips twisted up like she was trying not to say something.

"What, Ki?" She burst out laughing, and I did, too.

"How you know I had something to say?"

"Because yo' mouth kept twisting up like you was having a stroke," I said, still laughing.

"I was trying to have a serious face, leave me alone. But, no, seriously, I ain't tell you this before, but Miranda's ass hired somebody to kill me that night of yo' party." I jumped up from my seat, and my blood was boiling. I didn't know what was wrong with that ditzy bitch, but she was getting herself in some shit she didn't want to be a part of.

"Where the bitch at?"

"I don't know. Me and Banks had people out looking for her, but it seems like her and her mama moved. As long as she stays gone, then I don't care, but the second she pokes her head out, she gon' deal with me." Ki spoke so casually, but I could tell she was pissed on the inside because her eyes started turning colors.

"Well, you already know you better call me before you make any moves."

"Always. You know you number one. You didn't tell Uncle Law about the shooting, did you?"

I looked at her like she was crazy, then sat back

down in my chair to finish eating. "Hell naw, for what? All he gon' do is come back huffing and puffing about why we need to move to Miami by them, and I ain't got time."

"Maybe we should, shit, I'm tired of Chicago," Ki said, looking down at her hands.

"Are you serious?"

"Naw, I ain't going nowhere. It would be nice, though, or at least I need a vacation."

"I'm all down for a vacation, let me know! I need a do-over for my birthday anyway."

"No clubs. Well, you can go, but I'm not."

"That's fine." Ki had finally started showing. Well, it was a little pouch, but she said when she started show-ing, she wasn't being ratchet and going to the club. Even though if you saw her, you'd probably just think she had some gas to let go or something. I let her have that, though.

After I finished eating, I got dressed and headed to my studio to do some work. Since Ki said she had finished two weeks' worth of homework, I was going to plan us something fun to do out here. She needed some fun.

Chapter Seventeen
Kiarra

After Lo left, it was just Kenzie and me, so I decided to go to the park. I really didn't want to sit in the house, and I didn't have anywhere else to go. Once I got Kenzie and myself dressed, I grabbed the jogger stroller Lo had bought her and took it down to the door. After checking to make sure I had everything I needed for Kenzie and myself, I locked up and left out. The park was a block over, so I made it there in no time, and Kenzie was busy looking around at everything.

"Let's go get on the swing, mama." When the swing first started to move, Kenzie held on for dear life, and I had to laugh. After a while, she let go, and she kept looking up in the sky, so all her drool was going down her neck. Thank God, she had a bib on.

I kept Kenzie on the swing until she started to get fussy, so I went down the slide a few times, and she dozed off to sleep. I took this time to walk the track, and I hoped I could clear my head. I wanted to talk to my mom to see if she had gone through this when my dad died. I was legit afraid to fall asleep because I didn't want to have that dream again, but being pregnant, I couldn't fight sleep if I tried.

Kodi: Ki, are you busy?

Seeing the text from Kodi, I shook my thoughts away and continued my walk.

Me: No, wassup?

Kodi: I'm thinking about moving to New York, BUT it's for my career. I have a lot of people I could connect with.

I pouted a little because even though I had only known Kodi a little while, she was like a little sister to me and I was going to miss her if she left.

Me: Aaawww, it'll suck that you'll be gone, but I think you should go for it.

Kodi: I knoooow, I'll miss you guys, especially Kenzie! We'll try to come back often.

Me: We? Gerald leaving, too??

Kodi: Uh, yeah! Lol. He's not letting me go anywhere.

We continued to text, and I kept walking until my Apple watch notified me that I had walked 20,000 steps. It was only two in the afternoon, so once I got home and showered, I made a chicken salad for lunch and got comfortable in front of the TV, watching *Martin* reruns.

***

One week later...

"Hello?" I answered the phone out of breath as I rushed out the door to head to my doctor's appointment. I was officially sixteen weeks, and I was excited to see my baby today. My ultrasound appointment was right after my OB appointment; I hated that everything was separate.

"Hey, Kiarra, this is Melodee."

"Hey, girl!"

"I don't know if you're busy or not, but my best friend is having a striptease class at her dance studio tomorrow, and you and Lauren should come through."

"That sounds fun. Send me the time and address, and I'll check with Lo."

"OK, girl!" We got off the phone, and my phone beeped a few minutes with a text from Melodee. I sent a screenshot of the message to Lo and put my phone down in the cup holder. It took me fifteen minutes to make it to the doctor's office, and I was happy that it was empty today. I was called right back, and after my doctor told me I was tiny a million times, I was sent on my way. I walked across the street to the hospital and got checked in for my appointment. There were a few people scattered around the waiting room, and everyone seemed to be paired off. If I wasn't lonely before, I definitely was now.

"Kiarra Blak!" I stood up when the manly looking ultrasound technician called my name, and I followed her to the back. After confirming my identity, I laid back on the exam table with my shirt up and tried my best to get a look at the screen. It took her twenty minutes to get the pictures she needed, then she finally turned the screen towards me, and my heart melted seeing my little baby on the screen. My baby looked like it was going to be tall, and I know they could thank their daddy for that.

"Is this your first?" the tech asked as she handed me a towel to wipe the gel from my stomach.

"No, my second. I have a daughter who's almost eight months old."

"Oh, your hands are going to be full. I hope Dad is

around to help." See, this was where people pissed me off. She could've left that extra comment to herself. I didn't bother answering her as I snatched my pictures out of her hand and left. I mean, she didn't know about my situation, but I felt like she was judging me by her little comment.

I hopped in my car and had to do some deep breathing before I pulled off. Instead of going home, I went to Lo's studio to kick it with her for a while. I barely left the house anymore, so I wanted to enjoy the outdoors for a while longer.

When I walked into Lo's studio, I didn't see her anywhere, so I knew that meant she was downstairs with Adonis. So far, I loved Adonis for my bestie, but I had been wrong before, so I wasn't picking out wedding dresses just yet.

"Welcome to Chi Ink—oh, wassup, Kiarra?" Aaron spoke from behind the desk.

"Hey, how you doing?" I asked, giving him a tight-lipped smiled. I hadn't seen Aaron since he'd left my house a few days after the shooting, but he looked better.

"I'm good. If you looking for Lauren, she and Don went to grab some food, but they should be back soon."

"OK, thank you." I took a seat in the waiting area and tried to busy myself with my phone. Looking at the calendar, I noticed it was two days before father's day and my heart got tight. This time last year, we were finding out Kenzie was a girl. Now, it was just bleh! I didn't have a father or husband to celebrate, so it was going to be just another Sunday in my household.

"Hey, pumpkin, I ain't know you were coming,"

Lauren said, approaching me. I was so caught up in my own thoughts, I hadn't even seen when they came in.

"I was tired of being in the house, so I came to check on you." I stood and followed Lo out the door as she waved to Adonis and Aaron. Aaron was staring directly at me, and I caught myself staring back until guilt washed over me and I put my head down. This baby had my hormones all over the place, and I was thinking things I shouldn't have.

Get it together, Ki!

"You hungry?" Lauren asked, digging into her Jerk Villa bag.

"Nah, I'm good. What you doing tomorrow?"

Lauren looked up from her food and raised one of her eyebrows at me. "Why?"

"Melodee invited us to a striptease class and you coming," I said, rolling my neck at her.

"I know how to take my clothes off already, so what am I being taught?"

"Just be ready when I come get you tomorrow," I said, standing up and grabbing my purse.

"Damn, where you going?"

"Home. Love you!" I heard her smack her lips as I made my way out the door and I laughed. I knew I said I was tired of sitting in the house, but that was my comfort place, and I couldn't wait to get back in my spot on the couch.

Chapter Eighteen
Lauren

Kiarra was petty for that little three-second visit she had just done. She was lucky I had some work to do, or I would've made her ass stay. It seemed like the summertime was the busiest for me, but I—nor my bank account—wasn't complaining at all.

Ding!

The sound of the front doorbell chiming snapped my head up, and I saw Banks walking his ass in.

"What you doing here?" I asked, coming from behind my desk.

"Damn, is that how you greet your customers?" I looked at him with a 'yeah, right, nigga' face and he laughed. "No, for real, I'm here on business."

"What do you want?"

"Me and Kodi shooting our video for our latest song and we need your services."

"So, why Kodi didn't let me know that because we talk every day." Shit, we had talked this morning.

"I don't know, maybe she thought you'd say no." He shrugged and sat in one of the chairs in my waiting area.

"So, she sent *you* to come ask? I highly doubt that one."

"Look, it's gon' be in Jamaica."

"Okaaaay??" I mean, Jamaica is lovely, but did I really want to be in another country with him?

"And I'll pay double what you usually charge, plus pay for your flight and hotel."

"So, my entire trip will be on you?" I asked to clarify. He shook his head yes, and I stood with my hand under my chin like I was thinking about it. "Email me the details, and I'll see if my schedule is clear that day."

"A'ight, cool. Thanks, Lo." He stood up to hug me, and I held my hand out for him to shake.

"Don't thank me yet. Now, I have some work to do, you can see yourself out."

I took my seat behind my desk and woke up my computer screen. I watched Banks leave from my peripheral vision, and when I saw he was gone, I got my phone out to send Adonis a text.

Me: You ever been to Jamaica?

I hoped Banks didn't think I was coming alone.

***

The next day...

Yesterday, after Banks had sent me the details for his video, I extended the invitation to Adonis. After hearing his mouth all night about how he didn't want to be in another country with that nigga, he finally agreed to go. I was going to ask Ki when she came to get me because we were just talking about a vacation, and this would be the perfect spot. I just had to convince her to come with me.

Ki: Come on, I'm outside!

Speak of the devil. I grabbed my gym bag, phone, and keys and left out.

"Heyyy, you look cute," I said, admiring Ki. Her face was glowing, and she didn't look stressed like she usually did.

"Thanks, boo. I decided to comb my hair yesterday, and I actually slept through the night."

"That's good. You know you need your rest, especially with that crazy Kenzie. I can't believe somebody so small is so bad."

"Leave my baby alone, she is not bad," Ki said, laughing. I looked at her sideways, and she started laughing even harder. We pulled up to the Chicago Divas Dance studio and got out the car together.

"Oohh, this is Melodee's friend's studio? These girls be killing it. I'm ready to learn some moves. Shit, she could put me on the team." Kiarra laughed at me, but I was dead serious. People always thought I was younger than what I am, so I would blend in perfectly.

"I'm not about to play with you. Please don't go in here acting a fool, I don't wanna get put out."

"Girl, I know how to act, forget you." We walked into the studio and were greeted by Melodee. There were a bunch of poles set up, and I was happy I had come. Adonis' birthday was coming up, and I was going to make it a special one.

"Heyyy, thanks for coming. Let me introduce y'all to my best friend and the lady of the hour, Karter. Karter, this is Lauren and Kiarra," Melodee said, pointing to the girl next to her. Karter shook our hands and smiled from ear to ear. She looked cute, dressed simply in jean shorts, a tank top and some heels.

"Thank y'all for coming. We'll be starting soon, so pick a spot in front of the mirror." Karter pointed us to where we were going to be, and I followed Ki to the corner. There were a few other females in here, and I knew they were about to embarrass the hell out of themselves. Some of these hoes could barely walk straight, and they thought they were about to be in here like the next Blac Chyna. This was about to be fun.

Chapter Nineteen
Kiarra

Baby, would you mind touching me?
Ever so slowly. You're making me, quiver.
Baby, would you mind undressing me?
Making me feel sexy. While in the moment...

I was sitting here with my mouth open, watching Karter do all these flips and tricks on the pole. Janet Jackson's song "Would you Mind" played in the background, and I swear it made everything look a hundred times sexier. I could definitely see why Karter had that big rock on her finger. Shit, I was ready to marry her ass myself. Karter was giving Aliya Janell a run for her money right now.

"Ki, who she think about to do all that?" Lo whispered in my ear, and I had to move away from her before she started acting crazy. When Karter was done with her dance, she had everyone line up, and I chose to sit this one out in case my upper body strength was not what I thought it was. I was not trying to bust my ass and end up in somebody's hospital today.

"OK, when the music starts, everyone follow me. I'll go over it a few times, so don't worry," Karter said, then started the music. The way Lo rolled her body and bit her lip, I knew if she was doing this for Adonis, she was going to end up pregnant. I took Lo's phone out and started recording her because I knew she was going to want to watch this later.

"I hope you ain't get that other girl in my video." Lo came walking up to me all loud, and I had to put my hand on my head.

"Shut up, girl. No, it's just you." The girl must've heard her because she was lowkey mugging Lo now.

"What I gotta shut up for? Shit, she looked a fool. I hope she can suck a mean one, because if she does THAT for her man... he gon' pack up and leave her ass."

"Bihh!" I turned around, and Melodee was dying laughing in the girl's face. Karter was next to her, shaking her head and apologizing to the girl as she pushed Melodee away. I was glad someone understood my struggle of having a best friend who didn't care about what came out their mouth.

"Mel, you need to stop. I think you hurt her feelings," Karter said. She had her hands on her hips because Melodee and Lauren were still laughing.

"OK, Karter, I'm done. That was funny, though," Melodee said, still holding her stomach.

"This was fun. I know my man gon' love all that. I know exactly when Imma do it, too," Lo said.

"I'm glad y'all had fun. The next time we have something, I'll make sure to hit y'all up."

I exchanged numbers with Karter and Lo got their numbers too before we left out. We got in the car, and Lo's face was in her phone, returning emails and texts. My phone chimed, and a message from Mama Roxy popped up on the car's screen.

Mama Roxy: Hey, Kiarra, as you know, tomorrow is

father's day, and we were going to go to Deontae's grave. I want to take Kenzie, but it's totally up to you. I want you to come with us, too.

I was stopped at a red light, and it was like my whole world froze. I hadn't been back to the cemetery since we had buried Tae, and I didn't know if I was ready for that.

Beep! Beep!

"Oh, shit." I didn't know how long the light had been green, but I sped off before these people started cursing me out.

"You good over there?" Lo asked, looking from her phone.

"Yeah... well, no... Mama Roxy wants to go to Tae's gravesite tomorrow."

"Aaawww. So, what you gon' do?" Lo asked me. I shrugged my shoulders and continued to drive. "Welllll, I got us the perfect vacation coming up."

"Where and when?"

"Jamaica, bihhh! It's the weekend after the fourth, and we can bring Kenzie and everything. You down?" Lo asked me, then went back to typing away on her phone.

"I don't know, it might be too much for Kenzie. I'll let you know, though."

I dropped Lo off at home, and I went home myself. After taking a long, hot shower, I grabbed my laptop and got comfortable on the couch. I had some homework to finish, so I needed to get that done before Kenzie came back home tomorrow, but I couldn't concentrate because I kept thinking about the message I had gotten from Mama Roxy. I knew it would mean everything to them if we all went together, so I was going to put my big girl panties on and go.

Me: Hey, Ma, I got your message, and I'd love to join you all tomorrow. I'll meet you at your house in the morning for church.

***

The next day...

"Whether it's moving on from a past relationship, past disappointments, or past sin, remember God has a plan for you. His plan for you is not in the past but in the future. Your old life is gone, and now it's time to move forward! Allow the love of God to compel you to keep going forward. Trust in the Lord! Cry out to God for help for whatever is bothering you. Say, Lord, help me move on, heal my heart, lead me closer to you, Father! You can't start the next chapter of your life if you keep re-reading the last one."

"Hallelujah!"

"Talk to 'em, pastor!"

Have y'all ever gone to church and it felt like the pastor was speaking directly to you? That was what I felt as I sat in the pew and Reverend Jackson preached about letting go and forgiveness. It didn't make it better that it seemed like every time he finished a sentence, Mama Roxy would pat my thigh and look over at me. I felt like I was in an intervention, but it was everything I needed to hear before we went to the cemetery.

After service, I stood off to the side as Dave and Mama Roxy spoke to damn near the entire congregation. I had ridden to church with them, so no matter what, I wasn't going anywhere.

"Sorry about having you wait, Kiarra, sweetie," Mama Roxy said as we walked out the church.

"It's OK, I'm not in a rush."

Dave opened his wife's door first, then helped me inside with Kenzie. The whole ride to the cemetery, I listened to Dave and Mama Roxy joke and laugh, and it made me dread this visit even more. Being around them only reminded me of everything I had lost and that was the last thing I needed.

"Is everything OK, Kiarra?" Mama Roxy asked, turning around in her seat. I was so zoned out, I hadn't even realized that we had made it to the cemetery already.

"Yeah, I'm fine." I unstrapped Kenzie from her seat, and we all got out the car together. Mama Roxy had blankets in her hand, and she laid them out in the grass for us to sit on. I watched as Mama Roxy cleaned the. After sitting in silence for a few minutes, Dave cleared his throat and began to talk.

"Hey, son. You see I kept my promise and brought Ki with us today. I know she's missing you more than anything, right along with little Kenzie. She's getting so big and getting into everything now, but I can't even get mad at her, especially when she looks up at me with those eyes, man. Anyway, we'll be back to see you next week." Dave wiped tears from his eyes as he stood up and helped Mama Roxy up as well. "We'll give you a minute, Kiarra,"

Dave said, grabbing a sleeping Kenzie out of my arms. I nodded my head, and they went back to the car.

I stared at Deontae's headstone for what seemed like an eternity before the waterworks started again. "I'm so sorry this happened to you, Tae," I said between sobs. "But, I promise I made him pay for what he did to our family, bae. I love you." I placed a kiss on the top of his headstone, grabbed the blanket off the ground and stood up. I felt a chill go down my spine and I just smiled because I knew that was my love standing near me. I was glad I had decided to come; I feel a lot better, and I would be back again... soon.

Chapter Twenty
Banks

"Let's do one mo' take, G!"

"Maaaaann, we been in this bitch all night, my girl waiting for me," Gerald said, pausing the music. I had been trying to get my mixtape done before we went to Jamaica for this video shoot, so I had been pulling a lot of ten-hour days.

"A'ight, man, we can call it." I hung the headphones up on the stand and walked out the booth. "Lil Kodi got you whipped, bro," I joked.

"Get yo' single ass outta here. It ain't about being whipped, it's about coming home to my girl at a decent time." I waved him off and waited for him to power everything off so we could go.

"I'll holla at you tomorrow, bro. Same time tomorrow." I dapped Gerald up and got in my car to go home. It was only a quarter to eleven, and I didn't have any plans for the rest of the night. I couldn't remember the last time I had gone in at this time. As I was headed home, I decided to try my luck and give Lauren a call. The phone rang, and I thought the voicemail was going to pick up, but Lo answered at the last minute.

"Why the hell are you calling me this late, Giovanni?"

"I'm surprised you answered. Yo' man must not be around." I heard her smack her lips, and I knew she was about to go in.

"Nigga, first of all, don't worry about where my

man at. You better go find out where yo' bitch at and get off my line."

"Damn, you must still love me. Why you going so hard?"

"What do you want, Giovanni? I told you to call me at a reasonable time. Now, if you don't want nothing, I gotta go." Her little rude ass hung up and didn't even let me get another word in. I didn't feel like going in the house just yet, so I hit up the last person I should be talking to: Nicki.

Me: You up?

Nicki: Yeah, the front door is open.

Once I got that come through text, I bust a U-turn and headed to Nicki's house. It took me about fifteen minutes to make it, and just like she said, the door was open. I had my .45 in my hand as I walked through the house; couldn't be too careful. Nicki jumped when she saw me and her towel dropped to the floor.

"What the hell? Why do you have a gun?" she asked, holding her chest.

"I always got a gun. Come here," I motioned with my finger, and she sauntered over to me. Nicki tried to kiss me on my lips, but I dodged that shit and muffed her head back. "Fuck is you doing?"

"My bad, baby, I forgot," Nicki said, kissing my neck. She made her way down to my third leg and blessed me with that awesome jaw game. Nicki might not be worth shit, but I was sure she could end a war with her throat alone.

"Sssss, fuuucckkk!" Nicki took my member into

her mouth, and I felt the head of my dick tickling her tonsils. My toes were balled up so tight, I heard all ten of them bitches pop. I grabbed Nicki's ponytail and guided her at the pace I needed to get this first one off. When I felt the tightening in my stomach, I pumped even faster and let my kids shoot down her throat. "Aaarrgghh, shit. Get up."

Wiping her mouth, Nicki got up slowly and walked over to the couch. She bent over, giving me the perfect view of that kitty, and I made sure I strapped up before I went in.

"Mmmm, yessss! Aaahh!" Nicki screamed and moaned like somebody was killing her, and that shit was getting on my nerves, so I sped up my stroke until I released in the condom. While Nicki was laying on the couch, breathing like she had just run a marathon, I put my clothes on.

"Come lock up." Before she could start with her nagging, like she always did when I was getting ready to leave, I left out the door and jogged to my car. For some reason, I checked my phone, hoping Lo had called me back or sent a text, but of course, she hadn't done any of that. I was still hopeful I was going to get my girl back, I just had to plan something big in Jamaica.

CHAPTER TWENTY-ONE
Lauren

"That nigga gon' make me fuck him up," Adonis huffed from beside me. I knew it was coming the second I saw Banks' name pop up on my screen.

"Bae, it's not that serious," I assured him.

"You still be talkin' to that nigga, Lo?"

"Nooo, I don't still talk to *that nigga*, Adonis," I responded, rolling my eyes to the ceiling.

"Don't do that."

"No, YOU don't do that. If I wanted to be with him, I would be, but I'm here with yo' long head ass, right?"

"Watch yo' mouth." Adonis laughed and playfully pushed me away from him.

"Naahhh, answer the question. Am I here with yo' long head ass or not?"

"It's the principle, though. There's no reason for your ex to be calling you this late, whether it's business related or not."

"Goodnight, Adonis." I got comfortable on his chest and he was still huffing and puffing about the Banks shit, I guessed.

"Either you check him, or I will." Instead of responding, I laid with my eyes closed so he'd get the hint to shut up and go to sleep. I was tired from running around all day, and the last thing I was about to do was argue with him about somebody I didn't care about anymore. This had me rethinking this Jamaica trip.

The next morning, I was up early so I could go to Ki's doctor appointment. I would've stayed my ass in bed, but we were supposed to find out what she was having, and I couldn't wait. Adonis dropped me off at Ki's house, and she was already waiting in the car.

"What you in here pouting about?" I asked Ki, sliding into the passenger seat.

"I been up all night studying for this final and I'm tired as hell."

"Well, when we get back, I'll try to keep Kenzie busy so you can go back to sleep."

"Thank you soooo much, Lo. When you have some kids, you can drop them off to me anytime," Ki said, laughing.

"Don't speak that kind of evil on me! Don't get me wrong, I love kids when I can give 'em back to their respective owners, but I'm not ready yet."

"You're almost thirty, Lo. You don't wanna be fifty tryna chase around a newborn."

"I just made twenty-six, stop trying to make me old. Besides, I could always take one of yours when I'm having baby fever." I laughed, and Ki just shook her head at me.

When we made it to the doctor's office, I carried Kenzie inside, and we waited for Ki to get checked in. She was called back right away, and I stayed in the waiting room with Kenzie until they were ready to do the ultrasound.

Banks: Yo, can we talk?

I rolled my eyes at the text from Banks because he was really starting to get on my nerves. When we were together, his ass didn't want to talk this damn much. Now, he had so much shit to say.

Me: Is it regarding this video shoot?

Banks: Naw...

Me: Well, no, we have nothing else to talk about. I said we could possibly be friends, but you're being disrespectful to my relationship.

"Hey, if you're here with Kiarra, she's ready for you to come back," a nurse informed me. I grabbed Kenzie and followed her directions to the back. Ki was already laid across the table, and I sat in the chair next to her as the ultrasound technician got started. I kept looking over at the screen, and when I saw the little winky between the baby's legs, I jumped up from my seat and started dancing.

"What, what is it?" Kiarra asked, trying to sit up and look.

"Nope, you said you didn't want to know, so don't try to change your mind now." I laughed at the dirty look Ki gave me, and so did the technician.

"OK, I'm all done. I have pictures if you want them." The technician went to hand Ki the ultrasound pictures, and I snatched them out of her hand.

"Lauren!" Ki yelled, folding her arms across her chest.

"Let's go, Kenzie, Mommy's getting ready to start falling out, and we don't need that kind of negativity in our lives," I laughed, grabbing Kenzie and power walking out. Kiarra claimed she didn't want to know the sex of the baby until she gave birth, so I was just following her wishes.

Kiarra pouted the entire ride back to her house, and it was hilarious. I didn't know why she was mad. She knew I couldn't hold hot water when it came to keeping secrets from her anyway.

As I had promised earlier, I kept Kenzie occupied and let Kiarra get a good two-hour nap. And, *man*, that was the longest two hours of my life! Kenzie's little ass is bad! If she wasn't pulling stuff off the tables and every shelf her little ass could reach, she was shitting all up her back. And they wondered what I was waiting for to have a baby. Tuh!

"So, did you decide if you were going to come to Jamaica or not?" I asked Ki as she fixed us something to eat.

"Yeaaaahh, I think Imma sit this one out. I don't really feel like being a third wheel. Besides, I gotta go on a hunt for the perfect building for the clinic."

"What happened to the one you had before?"

"The amount of work it was going to need would've taken longer than I wanted to wait. I need something where all I gotta do is paint and have all the equipment delivered. It's harder than what I thought, especially now that I'm doing it alone. But, I'm determined to have everything up and running before the year is out."

"You got this, babe. I know the last couple months

have been crazy for you, so whenever you need me to step in, just let me know."

"That's why I love you, you always got my back."

"Riding until the wheels fall off... then we gon' be like *The Flintstones* in this bitch," I said, laughing. Ki shook her head and handed me the burger she had made for me. I ended up spending majority of my day with Ki, then took an Uber home. Since Ki was not going to Jamaica, I was going to make Kodi go shopping with me. I needed to get something sexy because I was going to put the moves I had learned from Karter to use.

Chapter Twenty-Two
Kodi

"Is Ki coming to Jamaica with us?" I asked Lauren as we walked through the mall. She already had both arms full of shopping bags, so I didn't know what else she would need to get.

"Naw, she said she's sitting this one out."

"Awww, that sucks. How has she been? I feel terrible. I've been so busy trying to get my mixtape done, I've been a bad friend."

"She's better. I mean, I know she won't be back to her normal, happy self no time soon... but she's finally been sleeping through the night."

"That's good. I gotta make sure I go see her when we get back. Buuuttt, I gotta tell you something."

"Please don't tell me yo' damn sister coming out here," Lo said, stopping her stride.

"Girl, I know better than to have y'all in the same place again," I laughed. "But, that Nicki chick been popping up at the studio a lot, and I think she's coming to be Banks' leading lady in the video."

"Aw, hell naw. That nigga tryna have me in jail in another country. Banks better be glad I'm coming for you more than him because I would tell him to find somebody else to do the shoot. Shiiiit, I could go to Jamaica on my own."

"Well, I'm glad you're coming. I'm scared to fly, and I didn't wanna be the only female in the group."

"I'm not about to be kickin' it with that li'l entourage, that's why my man coming. Anyway, you ready to go?" I didn't know what type of dangerous game Lo and Banks were playing with each other, but I really hoped nobody ended up in jail, for real.

"Yeah, I want a pretzel from Auntie Anne's first." We walked to the food court, and I kept feeling like somebody was staring at me. When I looked around, my eyes met some skinny, dark chick who was standing with her friends but mugging Lo and me hard as hell. "Lo, do you know her?" I asked, nodding my head in the direction the girl was standing.

"Who?" She looked to where I pointed and squinted her eyes. "Oh, this bitch bold," Lo said, grabbing her phone out her purse and texting somebody fast as hell.

"Who is that?" I asked again because I was so lost.

"That's Church's dusty-ass baby mama. I owe that bitch another ass whooping," Lo fumed.

"Let's just go. We got a flight to catch in the morning. We can tag that bitch when we come back," I tried to reason.

"You know what, Kodi, you right. I'm trying to be a better person. Let's go." Lo turned to walk in the opposite direction, so I said forget my pretzels and left before Lo changed her mind. Since I had driven, I dropped Lo off at home, then I went home to finish packing. I just hoped Lo's crazy ass didn't go back to the mall looking for that girl.

When I walked inside, I heard music coming from the bedroom, and I went in there to see Gerald packing.

"Hey, baby, what you doing here so early?" I asked, wrapping my arms around his neck and standing on my tippy toes to give him a kiss.

"I ain't wanna be in there all night, so after they finished up with the one track they paid me for, I left. You look like you were swiping the shit out that card," Gerald said, pointing to the bags I had dropped by the door.

"It's not a lot compared to everything Lauren bought," I laughed. Gerald gave me the side-eye and pushed me off him.

"Go pack. We going out to eat, then I'm tearing that up when we get back." He smacked me on the ass, and I went to grab my suitcase out the closet. It took me about thirty minutes to pack up everything, and I sat my suitcases by the door. Since I had been running around all day, I took a quick shower and got dressed for us to go to dinner. I didn't think I'd ever been wined and dined this much *after* I had given it up. Every day, Gerald made sure he showed me that he loved me, and I just hoped this didn't end anytime soon.

SHORTY FELL IN LOVE WITH A DOPE BOY 3

Chapter Twenty-Three
Kiarra

"Ki, you knooooow how hard it was for me to walk away without touching that bitch. I don't think Imma be able to enjoy my trip." I had been listening to Lauren vent for the last fifteen minutes, and it was so hard not to laugh at her.

"Lo, baby, just relax. I'm seriously over the whole situation. Everyone is OK, and it's not worth the stress. Get off the phone, do a couple of woosahs and pack your bags. I gotta go look at this building, and I'll talk to you later."

"OK, boo, let me know how it goes." We got off the phone, and I grabbed what I needed before I got out the car with Kenzie on my hip. The building I was checking out was on 103rd in the Beverly neighborhood, and although it was not the best neighborhood, I liked the space so far, and I hadn't even been inside yet.

Bzzzz!

I was buzzed inside the door and greeted by a short, light-skinned woman who was dressed in a pencil skirt that hugged her curves. I was not in any way attracted to women, but I appreciated a big booty like the next person. "Hi! You must be Kiarra. I'm Chellie, we spoke on the phone," she said, holding her hand out for me to shake. I had to adjust Kenzie before I returned the gesture and shook her hand.

"Hi, it's nice to meet you," I said as Kenzie started to squirm in my arms. I knew she wanted to get down, but I couldn't have her tearing up the place before I could decide if I wanted to purchase or not.

"She is so beautiful, and I can see she's ready to roam, so I'm not going to hold you. Let's start the tour." I followed behind Chellie, and she gave me the rundown of the space. There were four rooms I could use as exam rooms, two bathrooms, and a kitchen area. By the time we made it to the garage, I was sold, and she didn't even know it. The only thing that was a problem for me was the price. They were asking for 900K, and for the location it was in, it wasn't really worth it.

"So, what do you think?" Chellie asked once we were done with the tour.

"I love it. I'm definitely ready to make an offer. I hope the owner is willing to negotiate the price, though."

"I'm sure they will. I'll give you the papers to fill out, and I can reach out once we're all done here." I took the papers from Chellie and quickly filled them out. "I'm going to go over everything, and you should hear from me by next Friday, if not sooner. Enjoy your weekend."

"Thanks again, Chellie." I left out feeling good and was ready to start ordering equipment.

When we got home, I got Kenzie changed, fed and settled in her playpen. I was exhausted, and I needed at least an hour of peace.

"Da-da-da-da!" Kenzie yelled as she banged her toys together. That had been her first words, and I couldn't lie, I was jealous. Sometimes I stared at Kenzie and wondered if she missed Tae as much as I did. I knew she was too young to actually grasp the fact that her daddy was gone, but it was a thought.

I watched Kenzie until she played herself to sleep, and I thanked the Lord for that. Getting up, I went to the kitchen to prepare my dinner and to call and check on my mama. I hadn't talked to her in a few days, and I missed her.

"Hello?" She answered on the second ring, and her background was loud, like she was out.

"Hey, Ma, what you doing?"

"Nothing, cooking dinner. Hold on, Chubbz. Vince, are you deaf? Turn the TV down!" she yelled, then her background got quiet. "I swear that man is deaf. Anyway, what you up to?" she asked me.

"Nothing. I just got in from looking at another building not too long ago. I can't wait until everything is final."

"That's what I wanted to speak to you about. How are you going to run a business, take care of two small babies, and take care of yourself?"

"I'll figure something out when the time comes. Women do it all the time, and I'm no different."

"I don't care about other women, I'm talking about you. You have to take care of yourself, too."

"I know, mommy," I said, defeated. I knew better than to argue with my mama, so I just left it alone.

"We've been talking about moving back anyway so I might need a job," she said, laughing.

"Are you serious?" I got excited. I didn't want her to leave, to begin with, but at the end of the day, she was going to do what she wanted.

"Girl, yeah. Miami is cool and all, but I miss home. Plus, even though you're too stubborn to admit it, you're gonna need my help," she said, and I smiled. We talked for a little longer before she got off the phone to eat. I made myself a salad, and I joined Kenzie in the living room. This year had been really shitty to me, but it was up to me to change it around, and that was what I set out to do.

Chapter Twenty-Four
Lauren

"Yaassss, look at this house. I don't think I wanna go home," I said, walking through the vacation house we had rented for our stay. Banks' ass had a hotel room for me, but I wanted to be as far away from him and that Nicki bitch as I could. Shit, it was bad enough we were on the same damn plane. That bitch really thought she was winning with the way she was holding on to Banks' arm.

"This shit is decent, and we can do some thangs in that jacuzzi tonight," Adonis said from behind me. He wrapped his arms around me and pulled me back until I was leaning against his chest. His Ferragamo cologne entered my nostrils, and I felt a puddle forming in my panties. I felt his dick jump against my butt, and I knew he felt like I did. There was something about being in Jamaica that made me just want to bust it open all over the island.

"We ain't gotta wait till tonight," I said, turning around and smirking at him. I had on a sundress, so I lifted it up, and his hands went right to my ass. Adonis picked me up, so I wrapped my legs around his waist and attacked his lips. He started walking, so I held on to his neck in case this nigga dropped me, and he sat me on the cold-ass counter. Adonis snatched my boy shorts off and threw them on the floor. I wanted to snap on him until he kneeled and started planting kisses from my thighs up to my kitty, then everything was right in Lauren's world. He started sucking on my clit, and I couldn't take it, so I attempted to push his head back. Adonis smacked my hands away, then pinned them over my head. I kept opening and closing my mouth, but no words were coming out.

"This shit tastes good, bae." Adonis spoke into my honeypot, and the vibration from his voice sent me over the top, and I came all over his tongue. He wanted to play and keep going, knowing I couldn't push him off me with him holding my arms. I started squirming on the counter, and he stood up, smiling, wiping his chin.

"You play too fuckin' muuuucchh," I moaned as he rammed his dick into me. Adonis was giving me strokes that made me want to go kill any bitch he had ever fucked. He had the type of dick that would have me hopping out of bushes if he took too long to text me back. Yes, it was that serious.

We ended up on the floor, breathing like we had just run a marathon, and I didn't want to move.

"Come on, let's go see what we can get into," Adonis said, pulling me up and leading me to the bedroom.

"Shit, I'm about to get in that bed. I don't know about you, but I need a nap."

"Get yo' lazy ass in the shower. We not about to be cooped up in here the whole time."

"Huuuuhhh!" My phone rang, interrupting me, and I saw it was Kodi. "Talk to me," I answered, going through my bag to find something to change into.

"Since today is my only day I won't be swamped, do you and Adonis wanna go on this snorkeling tour?" I pulled the phone away from my ear and looked at it.

"Did you call the right person, Kodi? You know I'm

black, right?"

"I told you!" I heard Gerald yell in the background before he started laughing.

"I'm black, too, Lauren," Kodi said. I could just imagine her rolling her eyes.

"Barely!"

"Come ooonnn, Lo, it'll be fun," Kodi begged.

"A'ight, let me get dressed." I finally gave in.

"OK, I'll send you the address," Kodi said, then hung up.

"Where we going?" Adonis asked from behind me.

"Snorkeling," I said, shaking my head and going into the adjoined bathroom. I took a quick shower and tied my braids up in a ponytail. By the time I was dressed and ready, Adonis was waiting in the living room for me, so we left right out.

When we made it to the beach, all you saw was bitches with big booties and some sexy-ass shirtless niggas.

"Don't get flexed out here," Adonis warned. I got caught staring a little too long, and I had to laugh it out. We met up with Kodi and Gerald and went to grab all the equipment we needed for this damn snorkeling.

The water was clear, and it all looked beautiful, but I was still scared as hell. I wasn't the best swimmer, and I did not want to die out here.

"Y'all know how to swim, right?" I asked, looking around at everybody.

"Yeah," they answered in unison.

"A'ight, so if I look like I'm drowning, all you mothafuckas better save me," I said, waving my finger between the three of them. I made sure to look them all in the eyes so they knew I wasn't playing.

"I got you, baby." Adonis wrapped his arm around me, and we got on the boat.

The whole tour was about three and a half hours, and by the time we made it back to the beach, I was good and tipsy. After I found out there was an open bar, I said fuck that snorkeling and went to the bar. All in all, I had a good time, and I was ready to see what else Montego Bay had to show me.

After we went back to the house and got changed again, we all agreed to meet up at *The Pelican Grill* to eat. When I walked into the restaurant and saw Banks at the table with Nicki, I wanted to go somewhere else. Instead, I got us another table and was going to enjoy a meal with my man. Like I said before, I didn't want to go to jail in Jamaica, so I was going to try to stay far away from them.

Kodi: Are you coming? We're about to order.

*Me: I'm here, but yo' table looked crowded... *side-eye emoji**

Kodi: I forgot that fast lol... She is hella irritating, though.

I laughed at Kodi's text and put my phone up as our food came out. I stuck with what I knew and ordered jerk chicken, but Adonis got the curried lobster, and I eyed his plate, wishing I had gotten that, too.

"Get some, man," Adonis huffed, pushing his plate towards me.

"Aaawww, thanks, babe. You didn't have to do that." I picked up a fork full of the lobster and put it on my plate.

"Yes, the hell I did, stop lying." We shared a laugh and continued to eat. I had a few more drinks, and Adonis kept talking about how I was going to be passed out soon.

Shit, I was on vacation, I could pass out if I wanted to.

When my alarm went off at five in the morning, I regretted drinking all those rum punches last night. My head was pounding, and I wanted to stay in bed for a little bit longer, but since today I was technically supposed to be working, I got my ass up and got ready. Adonis said he wasn't about to sit and watch *that nigga* shoot a video, so he stayed back at the house, and I took an Uber to the set. The Villa we pulled up to where we were staying looked like a damn tent. I heard music coming from the backyard, so I went back there, and my mouth hung open. The pool that was back there took up most of the yard, and it even had a running waterfall over it.

"You didn't bring yo' bodyguard with you?" I heard from behind me, and I turned around, rolling my eyes.

"It's too early to be hating, Giovanni."

"I ain't hating on shit. I'm just saying that nigga be following behind you like a dog."

"Nah, my man just appreciates that he got a good one. But, speaking of dogs, yours is on her way over, and she looks a little mad," I said, laughing. I watched Nicki stomp over to us, and I prayed I didn't have to act my color this early in the morning.

Chapter Twenty-Five
Banks

"Gio, they're ready for us inside." Nicki brought her irritating ass up to me, and I wanted to smack her ass. When I invited her here, I wasn't going to lie, I was trying to be petty, but this shit was biting me in the ass.

"G, this my fuckin' video, ain't shit starting without me," I spat. "You being rude as fuck while I'm talking, though."

"That's my cue, bye," Lo said, laughing as she walked passed us. I didn't pass up the chance to get a look at that ass, though.

"Really, Gio?!" Nicki shrieked with her arms folded across her chest and her mouth twisted.

"Look," I said as I rubbed my hand down my face and looked at Nicki. "I'll still pay you for your time, but you gotta go."

"Are you serious right now? I come all the way to Jamaica, and you're just gonna send me home?"

"You ain't gotta go home—"

"But you gotta get the hell outta here!" I heard Lo say, laughing, then she stuck her head outside. "I have stuff to do, so you need to come on." Nicki turned around like she wanted to say something, but turned back around to face me instead. That was smart of her because I wasn't going to stop Lo from beating her ass this time.

"I apologize if I led you on, but this ain't it for me." I pulled a stack of hundreds out the Saint Laurent bookbag and held it out for her to take. Nicki acted like she was so hurt or offended, but I bet you her ass took that money and left.

After all the Nicki drama, I went inside so we could get this video started. The first few scenes were shot inside the house, and we finished up outside. I wanted to actually capture the beauty that is Jamaica in this video. The whole time we were shooting, I watched Lo move around, snapping pictures from different angles. She was nodding her head to the music, and I wondered if she knew this song was about her.

When we finally shot the last scene, the sun was going down, and I was ready to go lay my ass down. I caught up to Lo as she bagged up all her equipment, and I wanted to try to speak my peace one last time.

"Can I speak with you for a second, Lauren?" I used her full name because I wanted her to know I was being serious right now.

"I'm listening," she said, still moving around.

"I need your undivided attention, please," I practically begged. After she zipped her camera bag up, she put it on her shoulder and stared up at me. "I know I said the shit a million times, but...I'm sorry. I don't have an excuse as to why I did the stupid shit I did, and if I could take it back, I would. You got my heart, Lo, and I can't live without that." I reached out for her hand, but she pulled it back.

"That was a nice little speech and all, but did I have your heart when that bitch was sucking yo' dick in the studio? Did I have yo' heart every time you left out the house to go cheat? I don't fucking think so! So, save all that 'I'm sorry' bullshit. I thought we were better than that fuck shit you pulled. You knew what I had been through with the cheating and you know I wasn't trying to get into nothing, but instead of leaving me alone and continuing on with yo' hoeing, you kept trying until I finally gave in, then you turned around and did the same shit. Now you see I'm happy with a MAN who's doing what you failed to do, so you want to profess your love to me? Did you think that was enough for me to say F it, let's get back together? You know me better than that, Giovanni. I'll have your pictures back to you by next week." And with that, she walked away and left me standing there, probably looking as dumb as I felt.

"Pick yo' lip up, bro. We all fuck up... just gotta get it together for the next one," Gerald said, patting my shoulder. I just nodded my head, and we left, too. Since I couldn't have the one I wanted, I would just run through the ones I didn't. Say what you want, but this was how I coped with pain.

Chapter Twenty-Six
Lauren

"What's wrong with you?" Adonis asked, taking my bags from me. He had come to pick me up from the video shoot, and I was more than ready to go back home now.

"Nothing," I said in a flat tone. I was really irritated because Banks wanted to keep up with his bullshit. I hated niggas who love you so much when you move on from their ass, knowing damn well they were the reason y'all weren't together.

"So why yo' face over there all balled up?"

"Because I'm tired and hungry. What we about to eat?" I asked, trying to change the subject.

"I got something set up for you when we get back to the house," Adonis smirked. He knew I didn't like surprises, and it seemed like he was driving slow on purpose. "Put these on." He handed me a blindfold, and I looked at him like he was crazy.

"Aw, hell naw, you on some bullshit." Adonis laughed, and I tried to give the blindfold back.

"Come on, man, put it on. Don't ruin the night." Reluctantly, I put the blindfold on as we pulled up to the house. I heard Adonis get out the car, and my door opened seconds later. Adonis took my hand, and I got out the car.

"Don't leave my camera in the car," I said, trying to take the blindfold off to see if he had it, but he smacked my hand down. That camera had cost me damn near fifteen thousand dollars, and I didn't care where you were, niggas steal.

"I got it, just walk."

Adonis still had one of my hands as he led me through the house. "We going up the stairs now," he warned. My heart was beating fast because I didn't know what the hell he was getting ready to do. Finally, he uncovered my eyes, and I stood in the bathroom. There was a line of rose petals from the door to the jetted tub that was in the middle of the room. The tub was filled with bubbles and had a tray with chocolate-covered strawberries and a bottle of wine on the edge.

"Aaawww, you did all this for little ol' me? Thank you, baby," I said, giving him a kiss. Adonis made the kiss deeper, and he slowly started taking my clothes off.

"You know it's all for you, now get in," he said aggressively, then gave me a slap on the ass. I did as I was told, and the water was so perfect; not too hot and not too cold.

"Mmmm, you not gon' come in with me?" I moaned, taking a bite of a strawberry.

"When you doing all that, hell yeah I'm getting in." Adonis quickly stripped out of his clothes and slid in behind me. He had his arms wrapped around me, and I laid my head back on his chest, listening to his heartbeat. We fed each other the strawberries, and I drank the wine because Adonis swore it was a girly drink.

"Let's take a shower before I get too drunk," I said, standing up and stepping out of the tub. I always had to take a shower after a bath, or I still felt dirty.

We ended up having a quickie in the shower, then

he told me we had to hurry up before the food got cold. Shit, he should've started with the food. While Adonis was setting up the food downstairs, I slipped on one of the lingerie sets I had bought when I went to the mall with Kodi. I was going to turn some tricks tonight. Ladies, show your man you appreciate him, just like you want him to show you the same. I can't say it'll prevent them from cheating, but it'll have them thinking twice if you do it right.

"Damn, you were up there for twenty minutes to come back in a robe? Did you have to make it?" Adonis complained the second I came downstairs.

"Shut up." He pulled my chair out, and I sat down. When he pulled the lid off the plate, my mouth watered. There was a big-ass steak on my plate, and I couldn't wait to dig in. We ate in silence... well, sort of. Forks scraping and Adonis licking his fingers could be heard. When I was done, I had to sit and let it digest before I could move.

Adonis played music in the background, so I took his phone and turned to the song I wanted to play. As Tank's single "Nothing On" started to play through the speakers, I got Adonis set up in a chair in the middle of the room. When Tank started singing, I slowly took my robe off, and Adonis bit his lip so hard, I thought he was going to draw blood. I was having fun with my striptease, and every time he tried to reach out and touch me, I smacked his hand down.

By the end of the song, I was in his lap, and we were wrestling with our tongues. The music kept playing, but when "Only One" came on, Adonis pulled back from me and started laughing.

"Yo, Bro is singing about a stripper," he said, still laughing.

"What?"

"Tank's gay ass is in love with a stripper."

"And what does that have to do with what we got going on right now?" I asked, getting off his lap.

"Nothing, I'm sorry, baby." He tried to pull me back to him, and I moved back. "Come on, stop playing."

"Naw, I ain't playing. You so fascinated with Tank and his stripper, go holla at him—ahh!" I called myself trying to talk shit and walk off, and he snatched me up and had me pinned against the wall.

"Stop playing with me, Lauren," he spoke into my ear, and I felt the floodgates opening between my legs.

"I'm sorry, daddy," I purred. Adonis didn't know, or maybe he did, but I loved when he got all aggressive and shit.

He carried me to the room, and we went at it all night. We were set to leave tomorrow, and this was the best way to end our mini vacation.

Chapter Twenty-Seven
Kiarra

"Underestimation of a person's intelligence, strength and aggression just makes you less prepared. Expect anything from anyone."

That was something my dad had beat into me during one of our "lessons," and that was all that went through my head as I followed Miranda around. After Lo told me that she had seen her, I had every intention of letting it go and moving on with my life, but I tossed and turned all night, and all I could think about was how she had tried to take me away from my child. I felt like after Maine's body was found, she would get the hint that this wasn't a battle she wanted, but I guess she wasn't that smart after all because she tried to hire someone else to do her dirty work. Thankfully, it was someone who knew Uncle Law, so they called to warn him, and after Law cursed me out for not telling him about the shooting in the first place, he told me he was going to have someone take care of Miranda. But, this was something I had to do myself, just like with Church.

This bitch was so stupid, she was out shopping and having a good time like she was untouchable. Her ditzy ass didn't even notice me follow her all the way home. I pulled my car right behind hers in the driveway and got out. I had pulled my hood tightly over my head, so I wasn't worried about anyone seeing my face. She got out the car and squinted her eyes to see who I was, I guessed, and when she realized it was me, she looked like she had seen a ghost.

"I heard you been looking for me, Miranda."

"W-what are you doing at my house? How do you know where I live?" she stuttered.

"Go inside."

"Hell no, and you better leave before I call the police."

Click!

I pulled my gun out and pointed it at her face. "I said get the fuck in the house, and if you scream, I'll have yo' brains splattered all over this nice car you're driving." I nodded my head towards her front door, and she turned around slowly. I snatched her purse from her hand and gave her the keys to unlock the door.

"You're going to kill me like you had Church killed? You just couldn't let him go," she asked, and I pushed her into the house. Miranda was all of one hundred pounds soaking wet, so my little push sent her to the floor.

I laughed maniacally and bent down so I was kneeling over her. "See, that's the difference between you and me. I didn't have anybody kill Church, I did the shit myself. You wanna know how?" Miranda stared at me with wide eyes, and I think she finally realized she had fucked up.

"Well, I'll tell you anyway. After I cut the hand off he used to kill my husband, I stuck my knife in his windpipe and watched him bleed out on the floor. See, I was a fool for Church, too, once upon a time, but unlike you, I got smart."

"I-I-I didn't know—"

"Sure you didn't. Did you know he hit me while I was pregnant and kept me tied in a basement?" She shook her head no. "Well, damn! Did you know anything about him besides how his dick tasted? Stand up."

"Please, you don't have to do this. I'll leave, I swear I'll leave," she pleaded as she slowly stood up.

"Oh, I know you're going to leave, but you gon' take this ass whooping with you." I punched her in the face and kept swinging until I got tired. By the time I was done, Miranda's eye was swollen shut, and there was blood leaking from her nose.

"I advise you to take yo' kids and yo' mama and get the fuck outta Illinois. If I even feel like you thinking about going to the police or coming back, I'm going to make you watch while I skin yo' whole family before I put a bullet in your head. Are we clear?" She nodded her head, but I needed to hear the words come out her mouth. "You gotta speak up for me, Miranda, I can't hear you."

"Yes... w-we're clear."

"Good girl." I left out the door and jogged to the car. I casually pulled off like I was supposed to be there and drove to the woods where I burned the car and hopped in my own. I hoped Miranda didn't make me regret not killing her ass.

***

"Hi, this message is for Kiarra. This is Chellie calling to let you know that everything is set if you still want to go forward with purchasing the building. The owners agreed to the price, and all you have to do is come sign the papers, and it's all yours. Give me a call when you get this message. I'll be in the office all day."

"End of message. To replay this message—"

I broke out doing the running man when I heard that message. When I hadn't heard from Chellie last week like she said, I was ready to cry, but now everything was finally falling into place for me. I hurried up and called Chellie back, and she answered on the first ring.

"Chellie speaking."

"Hey, Chellie, this is Kiarra. I was returning your call."

"Hi! Sorry if I called too early, but the second I heard back, I wanted to reach out to you. When do you want to make everything official?"

"I can stop by in the next hour or so, I just have to get dressed," I said, getting out the bed and going to the bathroom.

"That works great. I can meet you at the building so we can do a final walkthrough and make sure there's nothing you want them to change before it's officially yours. And I'll have keys for you."

"That's perfect, I'll see you then." I hung up and jumped in the shower. It took me thirty minutes to get ready, and that was a new record for me. I was glad that Dave had come and got Kenzie last night because that was one less thing for me to do.

When I made it to the building, Chellie was just pulling up, so we met at the door.

"Aaww, I thought I was going to see that pretty little girl today."

"No, not today, she's with her grandparents." There was something about Kenzie that made everybody fall in love with her when they saw her. I think it was the eyes.

After doing a quick walkthrough, I signed the papers, handed over my check and I was officially the owner of what would be my first business.

"I can't wait to see what you do with the place. Good luck on your journey, Kiarra, sweetie. Do you mind if I pray with you?" Chellie asked.

"I would love that." Chellie grabbed my hand and bowed her head, so I did the same.

"Father God, I'm coming to You to ask that You continue to bless this young lady, her family and her business. Keep leading her in Your righteous path, Lord. I don't know her story, but You do, and You led her to me for a reason. Give her grace to forgive all who have sinned against her, and lead her not into temptation, but deliver her from evil, for the kingdom and power and glory are Yours, amen."

"Amen." By the time Chellie got done praying, I was in tears, and she gave me a tight hug. "Thank you for that," I said, wiping my tears.

"No problem, sweetie. If you ever need anything, don't hesitate to call. Take care of yourself." After making sure everything was locked up, I hopped in my car and wiped the rest of the tears from my face. The first person I called was Lo, but she didn't answer, so I called my mama, and she answered, sounding like she was half asleep.

"Maaaa, get up! It's time to celebrate!" I sang into the phone.

"What we celebrating, Kiarra, and stop yelling in my damn ear."

"Sorry," I laughed. "But, I am officially a business owner. I just closed on the building, and it's all mine."

"Aaahhh!" She was screaming in my ear—after she had just told me not to scream in hers—and I heard Vince in the background asking her what was wrong. "I'm so proud of you, Ki. I can't wait to see it."

"Thank you, mommy. I can't wait to get everything up and running." I was smiling from ear to ear as I thought about how I wanted to decorate.

"I'll be down there next month, and I can help with whatever you need."

"OK, Ma, I'll let you go, I just wanted to share my good news."

"All right. Have my grandbaby FaceTime me, I miss her."

"She's with her other grandparents, but when she gets back, I'll call."

I didn't want to go back home, so I decided to take a drive downtown to do some shopping. I didn't really need anything, but I could do some shopping for the baby and Kenzie. I was mad Lauren still hadn't told me what I was having and was making me wait until this baby shower I didn't want to have. I could always do the ultrasound myself, but I was going to wait and actually be surprised. I had a feeling I was having another girl, and that was why she didn't want to tell me. But, as long as it was healthy, I'd be happy.

**

Later that night...
Ding dong!

"Who in the hell?" I was deep into watching this Dave Chappelle stand up when I heard my doorbell ring. I checked my phone for missed calls, and I didn't have any, so I didn't know who the hell it could be. I checked the camera app on my phone and saw Kim standing there. She was staring up into the camera, and she had her hands on her hips. I laughed and buzzed her in. I hadn't talked to Kim or anyone from the hospital since Tae's funeral. It wasn't intentional, but I couldn't bring myself to go back there.

"Now, I was going to come over here and start fussing, but now that I see your little stomach, I just wanna hug you," Kim said, then wrapped her arms around me. "Why haven't you answered your phone, Kiarra? I've been worried. I had to wait until I had some vacation days to come pop up on you."

"I'm sorry, it's been so crazy. I've just been trying to take care of everything. I'm glad you came over, though."

"I know, how are you doing? Where's my baby that you been keeping from me?" she asked, looking around.

"She's with her grandparents right now, but I've been a lot better. It was tough to deal with at first, but I'm good. How are you, though? How's Miles and Mila?" I got comfortable on the couch, and she did, too.

"They're good, breaking my pockets like crazy. I hope you're prepared to be broke," she joked. "What are you having?"

"I don't know yet. Lauren is planning a baby shower, and I guess I'll find out then."

"I'm surprised you didn't do the ultrasound yourself. You know how you are."

"Really? I am offended." I gasped with my hand over my chest, and we started laughing. "But, no, I'm really going to wait to find out."

"Well, make sure I get an invite."

"How's work going for you?" I asked, an idea popping into my head.

"I mean, it's the same as it's always been; late nights and long hours."

"I have a proposition for you." I paused for a dramatic effect, and Kim gave me the 'OK, hurry up' look. "I'm opening a clinic in a few months, and I'll need your help. You can work the hours the kids are in school unless you want to work later. As far as pay, just give me a number, and I'll make it happen for you."

"Are you like serious, orrr...?"

"I'm serious. If you want the position, it's yours. I

have the building, I ordered everything I need, and after a few upgrades to the building, we'll be set to open the doors after I have the baby."

"I think that is great, and I'm so proud of you! Of course, I'll come. I'll be stupid to pass up this opportunity."

"Thank you so much, Kim." We sat back and talked for a while until Kim had to go get the kids from their nanny. I officially had one employee; now I just had to fill the rest of the positions.

Chapter Twenty-Eight
Kodi

We had been back from Jamaica for a few days, and I was ready to go right back on vacation. Koryn had been blowing my phone up about coming, and I had finally given in. Gerald was going to be cooped in the studio for the next few days, so I decided to take this ride by myself. When I pulled up to my mom's house, I had to talk myself out of the car, but I was point three seconds from pulling off and going back home.

"I thought I was going to have to come get you out the car," Koryn greeted as I made it to the front door.

"I was coming," I simply said and walked inside. "Now, what's so important that I had to get over here so bad?"

"Well, your family hasn't seen you in a while, and we missed you."

"I find that hard to believe, but I'll go along with it for now. Where is the rest of *my family* if I was missed so bad?" The entire house was quiet, so I doubted anyone was here except for us.

"Krista is at work, and Mom should be back—"

"Whose car is that parked in front of my house?" My mom came bursting into the house, and she stopped when she saw me sitting in the living room. "Oh, it's *you*. What are you doing here? I thought you were too Holly-wood to come over here again." I rolled my eyes up to the ceiling, then looked at Koryn. Obviously, she didn't know I had been invited over, and I was ready to punch Koryn in the back of her head.

"I'm not about to sit here and listen to this." I stood up from the couch and Koryn grabbed my hand.

"Come on, let's just talk out our differences. We're family, and we need each other. Please don't leave," Koryn pleaded. "Mom, can you please have a seat, too?" My mom gave me a dirty look all the way to her seat, and I felt like a random stranger on the street.

"So, who wants to start?" Koryn asked, looking between the two of us.

"What did I ever do to you?" I blurted after a few minutes of silence.

"Here we go," my mom said, rolling her eyes. "Everything is about YOU, right, Kodi? The whole world revolves around precious little Kodi."

"I never said that, but you don't treat me like you treat Koryn or Krista, and it's been that way most of my life. What could I have done so bad as a child that made you hate me?" I felt so many emotions inside, I wanted to cry, but I was going to hold it in. I wouldn't give her the satisfaction.

"You wanna know what you did? You stole the love of my life! After I had you, your father acted like you were the only one who mattered. Everything was Kodi this and Kodi that, I was tired of it!"

"How are you jealous of your own child?! That is fucking sick!"

"You turned out fine. Look at you, all over the radio and TV. You should thank me."

"I turned out OK? Do you know I got my ass beat for YEARS! Tortured, starved, burned and stomped for the hell of it. After the first time it happened, I tried to come back home, the one place I thought I would be safe, and you pushed me away. I could've died!" I screamed with the tears I had tried to hold in now coming down my face.

"Well, it's not like it was my fault." She had the nerve to shrug it off like it was nothing, and I lost it. I jumped off the couch and flew into her. I let out all my frustrations on her, and if it weren't for Koryn jumping on my back and pulling me off her, I would've kept swinging until my arms fell.

"GET THE FUCK OUT OF MY HOUSE!" she screamed, holding her bloody mouth.

"Gladly," I spat and grabbed my purse. "Koryn, don't try to get me to come out here anymore, or *that* will happen every time." I stormed out the house and left the front door wide open. I jumped in the car and sped off. I had to pull over on the expressway because I was crying and my vision was blurry.

My baby: You OK?

Gerald's text came through, and it was like he knew something was wrong. I guess I wasn't texting back quick enough because he called right after.

"Hello?"

"You gon' just read my text and not reply?"

"It was literally a minute ago, and I'm driving," I said as I pulled off from the shoulder and continued my drive back to the city.

"How did everything go?"

"Terrible," I sighed. "The only thing I accomplished today was realizing how fucked up my mother really is, but I'm fine, and I'll be back soon."

"OK, meet me at the house. I got something for you."

"What is it?" I perked up quick, and I heard Gerald laughing.

"Just get here and see," he said, then hung up.

I started doing eighty on the e-way and was able to knock a good forty minutes off the usual two-hour drive. I swooped into the parking garage, and power walked to the elevator.

"Damn, speedy, I hope you ain't get no tickets in my car," Gerald said, laughing, then gave me kiss.

"Shut up, I didn't get no tickets. So, what did you get me?" I asked eagerly.

"Damn, you just couldn't wait. Let's go grab something to eat first."

"Whyyyyy? I'm not even hungry." Gerald didn't respond, he just took my hand and led me back out the door. I was pouting the whole elevator ride, and he was just texting on his phone like he didn't care.

"Stop pouting, here." He handed me a black velvet box, and I got excited thinking it was a bracelet I had told him I wanted, but when I opened it and saw a Lexus key fob, I was speechless.

"You got me a car?!" I screamed, jumping up and down. The elevator doors opened, and there was a silver Lexus LS parked with a big pink bow on it. I ran to it and opened the door, admiring the cream leather seats. After

I touched just about everything on the dash, I got back out the car and hugged Gerald around the neck.

"I guess that means you like it."

"Yes, I do. I love you so much, baby, thank you."

"You love me, huh?" he asked, looking down at me.

"Yeah, dummy, you know I do."

"Prove it then." Gerald got down on one knee, and I swear my heart jumped out my chest and was sitting on the ground. "The way we met wasn't ideal, but I'm glad it happened. You showed me nothing but love since day one, and I want to make this a forever thing. So, will you marry me?"

"Yes!" I cried as he slipped the ring on my finger. I was doing the ugly cry with my mouth open and everything. "I can't believe you did all this and you told me you had to work," I said, hitting him in the chest.

"Ow! Watch yo' hands, man. I'm not about to be in no abusive marriage and shit," he said, rubbing the spot where I had hit him. "Let's take yo' new ride for a spin." I got in the driver's side, and Gerald walked around to get in the passenger seat. We rode through the city, and it felt like I was floating on clouds. It felt good to be in a healthy relationship. I now see that God had taken me through what I went through with Gates to show me exactly what I didn't need in my life. Now, I was about to be someone's wife, and I couldn't wait.

CHAPTER TWENTY-NINE
Lauren

The last couple weeks, I had been working with Melodee to plan this baby shower for Ki, and it was killing me to keep it a secret. It had gotten so bad, I had to pretend I was busy with work so I wouldn't have to talk to her that much. Lawd knows it was killing me not to say anything, but today was the day, and I couldn't wait to see her face.

"Ki! Where you at, I'm ready to go eat," I yelled, walking through her condo. I told her I wanted to go out to celebrate her getting all A's, so she was all for it.

"I'm coming. Shit, it took me five years to put my shoes on," Ki said, coming out of her room. Her stomach looked like it had blown up overnight, but she was the same way with Kenzie.

"You better get some shoes you just gotta slide in and go about yo' day."

"That's lazy as hell, Lo," she laughed.

"Yeah, but I bet I won't be breathing like I just got done fighting when I put my shoes on." We left out the house and went down to my car.

"Oh my God, the world is about to end," Kiarra said, looking up at the sky. "I know Lauren Shardae Jefferies is not about to drive voluntarily?"

I smacked my lips and got in the car. "You not

funny, heffa." She was on the passenger side, laughing like she had just told the funniest joke ever. "You so irritating, Ki."

"OK, I'm sorry, I just can't remember the last time you actually drove when we were together."

"Yeah, yeah." I turned the radio on and pulled off from the curb. We made small talk as I drove to Chicago Dough, and I texted Melodee the entire time, making sure everything was in order.

Melodee: We ready, just waiting on y'all.

Me: Pulling up now.

"It smells so good. I can taste the baked mostaccioli already," Ki said as we got out the car. I held the door open and let Ki walk in first.

"Surprise!" everyone yelled at the same time, and Ki almost jumped out of her skin. She had her hand in her purse, and I had to grab it before she fucked around and shot the party up.

"Oh my God, y'all can't be doing that. I almost had a heart attack. Lauren, Imma get yo' ass back."

"Love you too," I said, blowing a kiss at her. As Ki greeted everybody, I took that time to admire the whole set up. There was 'Girl or Boy?' balloons everywhere, and the tables were covered with half-pink–half-blue tablecloths. I was glad I had picked this location because we didn't have to worry about food, and they had a full bar that I was going to take full advantage of.

As I walked around, my eyes landed on Banks, and I hoped he wasn't going to be on his shit today, especially with Adonis here.

"Wassup, Lo?" Banks said, approaching me.

"Hello, Banks, thanks for coming through. I hope you didn't come emptyhanded like the nigga you are."

"Naw, I hooked my fam up. Don't try to play me like a broke nigga."

"I didn't try to play you like anything, but anyway, enjoy yourself." I walked off and joined Ki, who was sitting down already. "Soooo, did I do a good job?" I asked her.

"Yeah, you did, everything looks good. I just wish you would tell me what I'm having already."

"Have patience, child, we still have games to play." Melodee had a lot of baby shower games set up so people could try to guess what Ki was having. The only people who knew were Melodee and me... and Adonis because I needed to tell somebody, and he had helped me with my gift for Ki. I knew she was going to cry when she saw it, but that was going to be a good sign.

"OK, guys! I want Ki to open gifts before we announce what she's having," I said, getting everybody's attention.

"Lauren, don't make me drag you outside by yo' neck. You better tell me if I'm having another grandson or granddaughter," Tt Melissa said, pointing in my face. The crazy thing was, I knew she was serious.

"OK! We can do that first, no need to resort to violence." I held my hand up in mock surrender and went to my car to get the bear I had gotten made to tell her what she was having. I handed Kiarra the box, and everybody crowded around her as she opened it. Blue confetti came flying out, and Kiarra instantly started to cry.

Chapter Thirty
Kiarra

"Why you crying, Chubbz?" my mom asked, rubbing my back.

"I'm so glad I'm not having another girl." Everybody around me laughed, and they all congratulated me. I stared down at the bear, and he wore a shirt that said Daddy's Little Guy on it. Tae's picture was on the front of it, and it was from the maternity shoot picture we had done last year.

"It was so hard keeping that from you, bestie. I thought I was going to die." I hugged Lauren and tried not to cry again.

"Thank you for doing this, baby, I really appreciate it."

"Un-un, she ain't about to take all the credit," Melodee said from beside me.

"Thank you, Melodee," I laughed.

After I was done with my crybaby episode, I opened gifts and cut the cake. This whole surprise baby shower was fun, and my baby had been blessed with a lot of stuff.

"Ki, don't cuss me out, but me and Adonis got tickets to the comedy show tonight, so Aaron is gon' take you home, OK?"

"That's cool, y'all have fun." I hugged Lo and said bye to everyone else. My mom ended up taking Kenzie home with her, and I was glad I had a few more days of

A. JOVA'N

peace before she came back, wrecking the house. Ever since she had learned how to walk, it was like a never-ending marathon in the house, and I had to baby proof the entire house. Kenzie was getting into stuff I didn't even know she could reach. One day after I had woken up from a nap, I called myself getting a healthy snack, only to find that every fruit in the basket had a bite in it. I couldn't even be mad because it was cute to see her little teeth marks everywhere.

"You got a lot of stuff. I know yo' li'l man is set for a minute," Aaron said, getting in the driver's seat and pulling off.

"I know, now I really have to get his room together so I can have somewhere to put everything."

"If you need some help, just let me know. You don't need to be doing all that by yourself."

"Thanks, Aaron."

"It ain't shit, just call it payback for you helping me that time."

When we made it to my house, Aaron unloaded his truck by himself, and since I didn't have a place to put anything, my living room was filled with crap.

"You tryna get this stuff together now?" Aaron asked after he brought the last box of diapers in.

"I don't wanna hold you up. I got it from here." He looked at me for a second, then took his jacket off and hung it up on the rack.

"Nah, I told you I got you. Ain't like I got shit to do tonight."

"OK, well, lucky for you, the room is empty al-

140

ready, but I have to put the crib together." Shit, I wasn't about to turn down some help twice. Better than me struggling and getting frustrated. I showed Aaron to the room and gave him all the tools he was going to need to put the crib together. I started arranging the boxes of diapers in the closet and hanging up anything that had a hanger on it already. As I was going through the gift bags, I came across the bear Lo had made, and I kept staring at Deontae's picture. He was supposed to be here experiencing this with me, helping me set up our son's room, not some stranger. Every time something big happened and I was hit with the realization that I was alone, I wanted to go bring Church back to life and kill him all over again.

"Kiarra!" I jumped when Aaron called my name, and put the bear on the shelf. I hadn't even realized I was crying until he handed me some tissue.

"Yeah? Sorry," I said, wiping my eyes. "Did you need something?"

"I was just asking if you had a drill."

"Yeah, I'll go get it." I walked out the room and made a stop at the bathroom to get myself together. It had been a while since I'd had a breakdown, and I knew it was my hormones that had me crying at the drop of a dime. After shaking my emotions off, I grabbed the drill and went back to the baby's room. "Here you go."

"You sure you're OK?" Aaron asked again, staring at me intensely.

"Yeah, I'm fine."

"You know, it's OK if you're not OK. I've been where you are before, I felt that pain, and I can see the pain in your eyes. If you want to talk about it, I'm all ears." He went back to putting the crib together, and I just sat and let what he said float in the back of my mind for a while before I spoke.

"How?" I asked, sitting in my rocking chair. He stopped what he was doing and looked back at me.

"How what?"

"You said you've been where I was before, and I just wanted to know what happened. Only if you want to talk about it, that is. No pressure."

"Oh." There was a long pause as he kept doing what he was doing, and I figured that meant he didn't want to talk anymore... until he kept talking. "I lost somebody I loved a few years ago, being young and dumb," he said, shaking his head. "It's not an excuse, but you know it takes men a lot longer to mature than it would a woman, and that was my problem. I had everything I knew I wanted in Layla, and I was still fucking up, thinking she wouldn't leave, you know?" I nodded my head to let him know I was paying attention, and he kept going.

"Well, one day, a chick I was fooling around with called and told Layla everything, and she let me have it. Layla was pregnant at the time, and she just kept saying how she was leaving and how I didn't deserve her, and she was right, I didn't deserve her, but being a nigga, I couldn't just let her go, so I begged her all night not to leave me. We went to bed that night, and I tried to use sex to help my case. I thought it had worked until I woke up the next morning and she was gone. I think I called her a hundred times before I got a call from her parents. She was rushing to get away from me and was in a head-on collision with a semi-truck. She was ejected from the car and was dead before the ambulance even got there. Her and our baby. I blamed myself for years—shit, I still blame myself sometimes, but I learned to accept it. I guarantee I never cheated again, not that I've been in another relationship after that, but it was a lesson for me."

"How long ago did that happen?"

"Almost seven years ago."

"Seven years? And you haven't been in another relationship since then?" I asked in disbelief.

"I mean, I messed with some females here and there, but a relationship outside of the physical? No."

"Wow. I honestly don't think I'll even want to be with somebody else. It doesn't even feel right talking about it." I shook the thought out of my head. I seriously think Tae was it for me.

"You're young, do you really wanna be alone for the rest of your life?"

"I won't be alone, I have plenty of family and my kids."

"But, at the end of the day, they can't give you the same love and affection that your significant other can. Trust me, it gets lonely, especially when it seems like everyone around you is in love and you just playing in the background. You'll want to find that one who'll make your heart skip a beat again."

I sat in silence as I thought about everything Aaron had just said. I felt like I needed to call my mama and apologize for giving her a hard time about moving on with Vince. I never thought that maybe she got lonely. My mind was on her replacing my dad, and I knew that was something that could never happen, just like no one would ever replace Tae.

"A'ight, I think this is nice and safe, but test it out before you put him in here. I'm not trying to be responsible for any accidents," Aaron joked, standing up. I walked him to the door, and he grabbed his coat.

"Thanks again, drive safe."

"No problem. Don't hesitate to give me a call if you need anything else." I watched until he was out of my sight, then I closed and locked the door. I didn't feel like doing anything else tonight, so I took a nice, hot shower and laid down with my Kindle and ginger beer. I'd get up tomorrow and finish the nursery.

Chapter Thirty-One
Lauren

"That shit was funny as hell, bae. I'll definitely go see them again." We went to the Tight Ship stand-up comedy show, and I think I laughed the whole time we were there.

"Mmm-hhmm." I looked over at Adonis, and he had that same stank-ass expression on his face he'd had all night.

"That's ugly, Don. What is yo' problem?"

"Shit." See, this was where niggas had me fucked up. If you were mad for whatever reason, you should've spoken up instead of holding it in and acting stank because that wasn't doing anything but making me have an attitude, too.

"Aw, OK." I wasn't even about to figure out what was wrong with him, so I left it alone.

"You tryna grab something to eat?" Adonis asked after we sat in silence for ten minutes.

"Nope, you can just take me home." I didn't care if I was hungry; I'd eat at home. I didn't need his funky attitude rubbing off on my food.

"So, I can't come to yo' house now, Lo?"

"Naw, you can't. I don't need all that negativity messing up my feng shui."

"Aw, yo' other nigga must be coming over?" I looked over at Adonis like the fucking fool he was acting like, and I wanted to smack him in his damn head.

"I'm not about to play this game with you, Adonis

145

Edward Price. If you got something you wanna get off yo' chest, you need to speak now, or forever hold yo' peace."

"A'ight, why every time that nigga Banks come around, you smiling in his face and shit?"

"First of all, I wasn't smiling in nobody's face. He spoke to me, and I spoke back. Is that why you been over there pouting like a damn duck all night?" I laughed. "Ain't nobody thinking about Banks but you, apparently."

"Stop playing with me, bro. I just don't understand why his ass gotta be every-fuckin'-where y'all go."

"It's not for you to understand; it's not even for me to understand. At the end of the day, he's Deontae's family, so that makes him Ki's family. Of course he's going to be around. I can't control that, but I apologize if me talking to him made you feel some type of way."

"I feel like you tryna be funny, but a'ight."

"I'm not, for real. I sincerely apologize, Adonis." We pulled up to my condo, and he tried to turn the car off, but I stopped him. "Naw, you and yo' attitude is going to yo' own house. Text me when you make it home," I said, kissing him on the cheek. I got out the car and watched him mug me the whole time as I walked to the door. Once I was inside, I heard tires screeching, and I shook my head. He was driving my car, so I knew he had done that petty shit on purpose, but it was cool because the second I needed to replace my tires, he was going to be the one paying for them.

***

The next morning, I woke up with a text from Ki

and a couple from Adonis. I read Ki's message first, and she had asked me to come help decorate the baby's room.

Me: OK with yo' pregnant ass. Give me an hour.

After I responded to Ki's text, I opened Adonis' text.

*Adonis: I'm sorry for acting the way I did. You know I love yo' short ass... call me when you get up. *kiss emoji**

I smiled when I saw his message and decided to call instead of texting.

"Good morning, beautiful." Adonis answered the phone, sounding half asleep.

"Good morning, and I accept your apology."

"Yeah, I know. It ain't like you had too much of a choice anyway. When do you want me to bring you your car?"

"I don't know, you can just bring it after you leave the shop. I'll be at Ki's house all day, probably. She wants me to help with the baby's room."

"Aw, a'ight. Well, let me get dressed so I can head out, and I'll call you back."

"OK, bye." I hung up, then got out the bed so I could get dressed, too.

It was the middle of October, and Mother Nature didn't know if she wanted to be cold as hell or hot as hell. Yesterday it was damn near in the seventies, while today it was in the forties. After I took my shower, I threw on some black and gray *Pink* leggings and a matching hoodie. I ordered an Uber to take me to Ki's house, and by the time I was fully dressed and ready, my ride was outside. It took all of five minutes to make it to Ki's condo, and I let myself in. I heard music blasting, and Ki was having her own little concert as she sang "Drive By" by Eric Bellinger and danced around the semi-empty baby's room.

"You stay on my miiind—ah! Shit, Lo, you need to say something next time. Yo' ass gon' send me into labor," Ki fussed with her hand across her chest.

"My bad," I laughed. "It's looking good in here so far. You put the bed together yourself?" I asked, noticing the baby crib in the corner.

"Naw, Aaron did it."

"Aaron who?"

"Adonis' brother, fool. How many Aarons do you know?"

"I was just making sure we were talking about the same person. That was nice of him, though. Did you test it out first?"

"Hell yeah, I put a few watermelons in there." I burst out laughing, and so did Kiarra.

"You tryna say my baby gon' be the size of a watermelon?" I asked, still laughing.

"No, but I had to check that it was sturdy, no matter the weight."

"So, did Aaron creep you out with his silence?"

"No, he actually opened up a little bit and dropped some knowledge on me. He told me about his ex who got killed in a crash some years ago, and I actually felt sorry for him like I didn't just lose my husband a few months ago."

"Yeah, that is sad. Adonis told me about it one day when I was tryna find out why I had never seen him with any woman. Shit, I thought he was a little undercover, but it turns out, he's just heartbroken."

"Really, Lo? I didn't get that vibe that he was gay."

"I mean, you never know," I shrugged. "I'm sure

there are plenty of men out here who don't 'look gay', but that don't mean he don't enjoy getting his booty tickled every now and again."

"Okaaayyy, next subject. I decided I'm not going to throw Kenzie a birthday party."

"Whyyyyy?"

"She's only one. I'm sure she won't remember it anyway. I think just some cake and ice cream with her family would be all the fun she needs to have. Then, next year, I'll plan something big for her."

"Aaawww, that sucks. Are you at least going to let her go trick or treating?"

"Who about to walk up and down the blocks with her? Not my fat ass! Maybe we can have a small Halloween party and invite the few friends I do have with kids," Ki suggested.

"That sounds cool. Don't be trying to cheat my baby out of a birthday party, she needs to turn up. How's everything going with the building, though?"

"It's going good, I just need to hire another doctor if I can, or it's gonna be just me for a while. My mama has been trying to take over, and I keep having to tell her to pump her brakes a little."

"Stop lying. You ain't said that to Melissa."

"I said something like it. Damn, why you gotta crush my little spirits like that?" she laughed.

We talked and laughed as I helped Ki wash all baby boy's clothes and put them up. His little ass had more stuff than me, and that was terrible because I had to use damn near every closet in my house to be able to put up all my clothes. One thing for sure, though, I didn't think Ki had to worry about clothes or diapers for at least the next year. Whenever I decided to start popping babies out, I needed to be set like this.

After we finished washing and putting up all the baby clothes, I helped Ki plan Kenzie's party.

"We can just have it here. I mean, her birthday is in two weeks; that's too last minute if you want to go somewhere else," I suggested.

"That sounds good to me. I'm not trying to do nothing too big, especially with all my money being tied up with the practice right now. But, I do want her to enjoy her birthday."

"A'ight, I'll get the cake and decorations, and you handle the food and invite all your mommy friends. Me and my baby gon' have matching costumes. It's lit!"

I stayed at Ki's house until Adonis came to pick me up. He had my whole back seat filled with different bouquets of flowers, and he looked at me with the puppy dog face when I got in the car.

"What?" I asked, putting my seatbelt on and turning towards him.

"You not still mad, right?"

"Naw, I've been over it."

"Bet. We got some making up to do."

Chapter Thirty-Two
Kiarra

After Lo left, I decided to do some homework and my discussion questions for the week, so I could get it out the way.

My life had been so chaotic, and I couldn't wait for everything to get back to a pace I could keep up with. If I wasn't doing homework, I was chasing Kenzie around the world or running around, making sure I had all the permits and licenses I needed before I could open the door to the clinic. Now, thanks to Lo, I had to try to find some friends who had kids to come to my baby's birthday party. So far, all I had was Kim's twins and Karter's son, who was a few months older than Kenzie, so it looked like there were going to be more adults than kids. Next year, I'd be more prepared and my baby's second birthday would be more organized.

I ended up falling asleep on the couch, and when I woke up the next morning, my laptop was on the floor. Thankfully, it wasn't broken because that would be something else I had to replace.

Getting up off the couch, I went to my private bathroom to empty my bladder and take a shower. I really wanted to take a nice, long bath, but since I was here alone, I didn't want to be stuck in the tub like one of those old people in the Life Alert commercial. I couldn't go out like that.

"Chubbz! You home?" I heard my mom yell, and I poked my head out the bathroom door.

"I'm in here!" I responded and wrapped myself in my robe. I had to remember to tell her that key was for emergencies only because now that she and Vince had officially moved back, she was going to try to pop up whenever she wanted.

"I came to bring this bad baby back to you. She's been driving me crazy all morning," my mom said as Kenzie reached out for me.

"Heyyyy, ma ma—"

"You bet' not try to pick her big butt up," my mama warned, giving me the death stare.

"My baby misses me. I was just gon' give her a hug." My mom sat on my bed as I got dressed, then I joined her. "What are you doing today?"

"Nothing, about to go get back in the bed when I leave here, why?"

"Dang, I can't ask my own mama questions no more?"

"Nope, you sho can't. If you start asking what I'm doing, that means you want something, and whatever it is, the answer is no."

"Not even if it's for your granddaughter?"

My mom made a face like she was thinking of her answer before she said, "What is it?"

"I'm throwing her a small party for her birthday—well, on the Sunday before her birthday—and I need you to do the food, pleeeaassee."

"Aw, hell, I should've stayed my ass in Miami if I knew you were going to be putting me to work like this."

"Thank you. I love you, we appreciate you," I said, laughing. "Kenzie, tell Nana you love her."

"Da-da-da-da!" Kenzie said excitedly in her baby language as she clapped her hands.

"Mmm-hhmmm, you full of it, both of y'all. What's going on with your practice, though? Do you have all your paperwork in order?"

"Yessss, Ma, I told you last time I'm just waiting to hear back from the DEA, then I'll be all set."

"I know I told you a million times already, but I'm so proud of you, Kiarra. This year hasn't been easy for you, but you been kicking ass and taking names. You are goals, baby."

"Thank you, but, Ma, don't say that no more." She playfully pushed me, then stood up.

"You're a hater, but I'm about to get outta here. Come lock the door. Call me if you need me." My mom left, and I went to the kitchen to find something to eat before my baby came karate kicking out of my belly button.

**

Later that day...

Kenzie and I were enjoying a nap when my phone started blowing up on the nightstand. I answered quickly when I saw Lauren's name, and I heard her snapping on somebody in the background.

"Hello?"

"Naw, you got me fucked up! I don't care who you are! Hello?"

"What is going on over there?" I asked, sitting up in the bed.

"This thirsty-ass police officer wanna pull me over, talking about I was speeding. I ain't never got a ticket in my life! Now his fat, baldhead ass don't wanna give me

my license back while he over on that walkie-talkie. I
HOPE YOU CALLING YOUR SUPERVISOR LIKE I SAID!"

"Lo, calm down. Where you at?"

"Over here in Oak Lawn. I was just tryna go get me
some ice cream, and his bored ass wanna mess with me."

"Ma'am, I'm going to have to ask you to watch your
mouth," I heard who I assumed was the officer say in the
background.

"And I'm going to ask you to kiss my ass and give
me my damn license back! Pumpkin, let me call you
back, I'm about to call my daddy." She hung up, and I
shook my head at my crazy-ass best friend. She didn't
care what she said, or who she said it to, and sometimes,
I wished she wouldn't do that, especially to a police officer with all the stuff going on with them killing black
people.

I laid back on the bed and waited for her to call me
back and hoped she didn't land herself in jail.

Chapter Thirty-Three
Lauren

These damn police officers thought somebody was stupid. First, he claimed I was speeding. I might have been going a little over, but still, he was too damn thirsty. I would've taken my ticket and gone about my day, but when he tried to act like I couldn't get my license back, that was when I had to show my ass.

"Ma'am, you are free to go," this fat neck ass officer had the nerve to say to me.

"Don't talk to me until your supervisor gets here," I said as I texted Adonis.

*Me: If I end up in jail, it's yo' fault for not going to get my ice cream! *angry emoji**

I looked up as another police car pulled up, and I got out the car. Officer Fat Neck tried to go talk to him first, so I politely interrupted whatever lie he was trying to tell.

"Excuse me, sir, I requested you to come out. How are you doing, sir? I am Lauren Jefferies, and this officer is refusing to give me my identification back."

"I apologize about that, Miss. Officer Malone, can you please return this lady's license back to her?" Officer Malone handed me my license, and I snatched it out his hand.

"Thank you," I said, rolling my eyes. "And have a nice day!" I got back in my car and pulled off with Officer Malone staring at me like he wanted to knock my head off, and I smirked at him.

My phone rang in the cup holder, and Adonis' name popped up, so I answered it through the car's speaker.

"Hello?"

"What the hell you talking about? Where you at?"

"I'm finally about to get my ice cream."

"What's taking so long?" I ran down the story about what happened, and he told me to stop talking shit to everybody and to get to. Adonis swore he was somebody's daddy sometimes, and I had to remind him I only had one of those, and his name is Lawrence.

After going to Cold Stone for my ice cream, I drove to Adonis' house, and I made sure I went under the damn speed limit in case thirsty ass was waiting on me to come back.

I made it to Adonis' house, and he opened the door, shaking his head at me.

"So, was yo' ice cream worth that $150 ticket you got?"

"Hush. If you would've got it when I asked, I wouldn't have needed to make that extra stop. I feel like it's only right that you pay it since it's technically your fault."

"Yeah, it sounded good, didn't it?"

"Wait until we get to Grandma's house. I'm telling her how you be treating me." Adonis' grandmother Lu loved me, and she told me every time I went over. She said I was a firecracker and she saw a lot of herself in me, and I took that as a compliment.

"You always tryna turn my granny against me."

"Don't be jealous, baby. Granny still loves you, she just loves me more."

"A'ight, well, see if Granny gon' pay that ticket for yo' ass." We shared a laugh, and I waited until he was finished getting dressed. Granny always had her big dinners on Saturdays instead of Sunday because she said she wasn't leaving the house on the Lord's day.

***

"There go my Lauren. I was just about to call you," Granny said as she opened the door.

"Hey, Granny, you know I was coming over." I gave her a hug, and I heard Adonis smack his lips.

"Dang, Granny, how you just gon' ignore me like that?" Adonis asked, holding his chest like it hurt.

"Boy, ain't nobody forgot about your big head butt. I been looking at you for the last twenty-eight years, it's good to see a new face," Granny said, then led us through the house. The food was already laid out on the table, and I was happy I didn't have to wait.

"Wassup, sis?" Aaron spoke.

"Hey, Aaron."

"How Kiarra doing?" Aaron asked, shocking me. I looked up at him, and my eyebrow rose.

"Why?" I didn't like people asking about my Kiarra. I mean, Aaron was cool and all, but he needed to chill out on my bestie.

"Damn, my bad, li'l sis. Don't kill me, I was just trying to make conversation."

"Who is that, some little girl you liking on?" Granny asked.

"Nah, Granny, it ain't like that."

"Well, it's about time you find somebody. You not getting any younger, and neither am I. I need some great grandbabies outta you two before I kick the bucket."

Adonis looked over at me, and I kept my eyes

forward. He was better off buying a dog than me having a baby right now. I still had a little more living and traveling to do before we started discussing having babies. And if Adonis was trying to hint towards some babies, he better have a ring in that pocket, or he better look somewhere else. Lauren Shardae Jefferies wouldn't be anybody's baby mama.

Chapter Thirty-Four
Kiarra

Well, it was official; I now had a one-year-old. We had to postpone her party because we both ended up sick this past weekend and couldn't do nothing. But, since she was back to running around the house, I had invited a few people over for cake and ice cream so she could enjoy her day. But, first, we were going to take a trip to the cemetery to see Deontae. It was a little chilly outside, so I didn't plan to be out here long, but I wanted Kenzie to be close to her dad again.

Thankfully, there wasn't any snow down yet, so we could sit on the ground without getting frostbite.

"Da-da," Kenzie said, reaching for Deontae's picture that was on his headstone.

"Yes, that's daddy, Kenz. He's not here with us anymore, but he loved you more than anything in this world. Never forget that, OK?" I was talking to Kenzie, but she just stared up at me like I was crazy and started grabbing my chain. "Our baby girl is one now, Tae, can you believe it? She's getting into everything, and I can't keep up with her sometimes. We finally got our little boy coming, and I decided to give you your junior you wanted. Deontae David Blak Jr. should be here in about four weeks, and I can't wait to see what he looks like. Well, me and Kenzie gotta go get cake wasted with the family, but we'll be back soon." I placed a kiss on the top of his headstone and walked to the car.

When we got back to the house, Lauren and my mom were there, putting up some decorations and cooking.

"It smells good in here," I said, getting their attention.

"There go my sweet grandbaby. Happy birthday, Snuckums." My mama picked Kenzie up and carried her to the kitchen. I knew she was about to sneak her some junk, but I didn't even have a problem with it today since it was a special occasion.

"How did it go?" Lo asked.

"It was good. I actually look forward to going, and I hate when I have to leave sometimes."

"That's good. I'm glad you're feeling better about it. I admire your strength, boo. Now, go get changed into your costume so we can get this party on the road."

I walked to my room and put on the Minion costume I had bought for the occasion while my mama got Kenzie dressed in her matching costume. Even though the party was put together on kind of short notice, Kenzie had fun, and she even got some gifts, which I didn't expect. My baby ate so much junk, then played herself to sleep, and I was grateful for that because Little Tae had been kicking my ass all night. I couldn't wait until this pregnancy was over and I was able to hold my baby boy, I just hoped he was a chocolate drop like his daddy.

***

The day after Kenzie's birthday, I had to go right back into business mode and go down to the clinic and make sure everything was together for me to open the doors in a few months. I had Melodee planning a grand opening for the clinic on the first of the year, and I was ready to finally have my business up and running.

I pulled up in front of the clinic, and I was proud to see the 'Blak Family Wellness Center' sign plastered on the front window. Walking inside, everything was set up, and it looked good, but it still felt as if it was missing something. I wanted some pictures or different paintings hung up to give it a more comfortable feel, so I called Lo to see if she had any pictures she wanted to sell.

"Hey, Pumpkin, my baby coming yet?" she answered on the second ring, and it sounded like she was in the car.

"No, not yet, unfortunately. What you doing?"

"On my way to get this head of mine done. Wassup?"

"Nothing, just over here admiring how the clinic is coming along. I need some artwork to hang up in here... it feels so dry."

"Dang, I literally just sold my last one. Just stop by the shop and ask Aaron to do it. He did most of the paintings in Chi Ink. I know he'll do it, especially for you," Lo joked. She told me how Aaron had asked about me the other day, and it was kind of awkward to know that.

"Shut up, heffa, you're not funny, but I'll stop by after I leave here."

"A'ight, let me know if I gotta put a foot on Aaron's neck to get him to do it."

"Girl, if he can't do it, then I'll figure something else out. You not about to bully nobody into doing stuff for me."

"How come?" Lo asked, and I had to look at the phone because she couldn't be serious right now.

"I'm not about to play with you, Lauren. I'll talk to you later." I disconnected the call and stuck the phone in my pocket.

After locking up and setting the alarm, I drove to Chi Ink. I hoped Aaron was there because I was ready to go lay my ass down before my feet started to swell. I found a parking spot close to the door, got out and walked inside.

Chapter Thirty-Five
Aaron

Ding!

"I'll be right with you!" I yelled as I cleaned up my workstation. I walked to the front of the shop and saw Kiarra sitting in the waiting room. I wasn't going to lie, she had been on my mind heavily lately, and I liked the vibe I got when I was around her.

"Wassup, Kiarra, you good?" She looked up at me, and her eyes lit up.

"Yeah, I'm good, but I need a huge favor."

"What you need?" I took a seat across from her and took in her beauty. Even though she was very much pregnant, that didn't take away from anything; she was naturally beautiful.

"I wanted to see if you could paint a mural for me inside the waiting room of my clinic. You're free to create what you want, but I want to bring a little more life to the walls. Of course, I'll pay you," she added.

"I got you, just get whatever colors you want and give me a call when you're ready."

"Thank you, I'll let you get back to work now."

"A'ight, and, Kiarra, don't hesitate to use my number if you need anything else."

"OK, thanks again." She rushed out the door, and I went back to cleaning.

Kiarra reminded me a lot of my ex, Layla, and I think that was why I felt connected with her. It wasn't that they looked alike because Kiarra and Layla were literally night and day, but the way they cared for people and basically wore their heart on their sleeve was the same. I knew all about Kiarra losing her husband—shit, I was busting guns with her when she found who did it—so a relationship was definitely not what I was looking for. Now, I was not blind, so of course, I appreciated a beautiful woman like the next, but I genuinely wanted to be her friend more than anything.

After cleaning and locking up, I left the shop to go check on my Granny. She wasn't getting any younger, and I tried to check on her a few times a week to make sure she didn't need anything.

"Hey, Aaron, baby. I knew I was going to be seeing you today," Granny said as she opened the door and let me in. I bent down to hug her short, 5'2 frame and gave her a kiss on the cheek. "I just got done making a sweet potato pie, did you eat?"

"I didn't come over here for all of that, Granny, I was just making sure you were doing OK."

"I told you and Don about fussing over me, but if you want to help me, go ahead and take that garbage out for me."

"I got you, Granny."

I sat back to chill with Granny for a little while, and my mind drifted off to Kiarra. I couldn't help but notice that every time she smiled, it never made it to her eyes. She was still hurting, and I didn't blame her. There wasn't a timeline on pain; I know it had taken me a minute.

"What's her name?" Granny asked, snapping me out of my thoughts.

"What's whose name?"

"Don't play crazy with me, boy. You got that same googly-eyed look you had when you met Layla."

"All right, I gotta go, Granny. I'll be by to see you in a few days," I said, standing up and kissing her on the cheek.

"Mmm-hmm, lock that bottom lock on yo' way out."

One thing Granny had always been able to do was read me like an open book. I was the reason me and Don always got caught doing stuff when we were younger. All Granny had to do was give me that look, and I had diarrhea of the mouth. My grandmother had taken Don and me in when I was ten, and he was nine. Around that time, our mom was more worried about chasing behind whatever boyfriend she had at the time than to care for us how we needed to be cared for. We would go days without eating or even having clean clothes, and that forced us to grow up way before we were ready to. When Granny found out what my mom was doing, she popped up at the house, whooped my mom's ass and made us pack all our stuff. It wasn't like my mom put up much of a fight because we didn't hear from her again until I was a senior in high school. By that time, I didn't need that mother figure anymore because I had Granny, and y'all see that lady is more than enough.

Granny bringing up Layla had put me in my feelings a little bit. That was always a touchy subject for me that I rarely spoke about. I had shocked my-damn-self when I shared that with Kiarra because the only people who knew were my family, and that was because they had to come dig me out of the hole I had put myself in after her death. Depression was real, and it could be crippling if you allowed it. I was just glad I had my brother and Granny there to help me through it.

My artwork was another thing that helped me. When I had a pencil, paintbrush, tattoo gun, or whatever, I let all my emotions out on the canvas and created a masterpiece. That was why I had agreed to paint the mural for Kiarra. Maybe my art could be healing for her as well.

CHAPTER THIRTY-SIX
Kiarra

Me: Hey, if you're not busy later, you can meet me at the clinic, and you can get a look at the wall I need painted.

After I sent the text to Aaron, I felt nervous, and I didn't know why. Well, let me not lie like that. Aaron made me nervous because he stared at me like he was reading my soul, and I hated it.

Aaron: That's cool...just let me know what time.

I texted him the address and told him to meet me there in two hours. I had a doctor's appointment today, so I was going to swing by afterward. Hopefully, this didn't cost me an arm and a leg, even though I knew it would be worth it.

Getting up to get a start on my day, I took a shower, handled the rest of my hygiene and got dressed. I didn't feel like cooking, so I stopped at Dunkin Donuts on the way to the doctor for a breakfast sandwich. I ate in my car before going inside to get checked in.

The office was packed, and I was glad when my name was called right away. After the nurse took my vitals, she left and told me to get undressed from the waist down. So, I sat on the hard bed, waiting for my doctor to come in.

"Good morning, Kiarra. How are you feeling?" Dr. Gibson asked, washing her hands and grabbing some gloves.

"I'm doing good, ready to have this baby."

"I bet you are. The last few weeks are always the worse. Your blood pressure is a bit high, so we have to watch out for that. Have you been having any contractions or any symptoms of early labor?"

"I've had a few Braxton Hicks contractions, but nothing too bad."

"OK, go ahead and lay back for me so I can check you." I laid back and tried to relax as she checked my cervix. This had to be the most uncomfortable shit ever, and I hated this part of the appointment.

"You feel like you're about one and a half to two centimeters dilated, but that's normal at this point in pregnancy. You could go weeks without any improvements, so don't panic just yet. But, if you have consistent contractions that are three minutes apart, or if your water breaks, then go right to the hospital. Do you have any questions?"

"No."

"OK, well make an appointment for next week, and I'll see you then. Take care of yourself." She washed her hands again and walked out the room, leaving me to get dressed.

After I left there, I drove to my clinic, and I saw Aaron's truck parked outside already.

"Hey, sorry if I had you waiting long," I said, unlocking the door and letting us in.

"I just got here, I wasn't waiting long," Aaron said.

I disarmed the alarm and went to the waiting room to show Aaron the wall I wanted to be painted. "I want this whole wall covered if you can."

"Did you get the paint already, or do you know what colors you want?" Aaron asked, pulling some measuring tape out of his pocket and measuring the wall.

"No, I was actually going to go get it today."

"OK, I could go with you, and I could get started today if you want me to," he offered.

"That'll work for me. What is all this going to cost me?" I asked.

"Nothing, it's on the house, just consider it a gift." I had to give him a side-eye.

"I'm not letting you do this for free."

"Come on, I'll drive," he said, ignoring me.

"Did you hear what I said?"

"Yeah, I heard you, now let's go." I shook my head and followed him outside to his truck. He helped me in the passenger seat, then walked around to get in.

Aaron drove to Lowe's, and it took me almost an hour to pick out a color I wanted, and I still ended up buying damn near every color they had. I was a firm believer in getting extra everything; better safe than sorry. When we got back to the clinic, Aaron got set up in the front, and I went to the back to lay down in one of the exam rooms. I told myself I was just going to relax, but I ended up falling asleep.

"Kiarra, Kiara, wake up." My eyes popped open, and Aaron was standing over me with a concerned look on his face.

"My bad, I guess I didn't realize how tired I was," I said, sitting up.

"You good? You were in here screaming."

"Yeah, I'm good, crazy pregnancy dreams. Are you done?" I asked, changing the subject. I didn't want to talk about all the dreams I kept having with Tae holding me, only for me to wake up and realize it was a dream.

168

"Not quite, but I got a client on the way to the shop. I could come back tomorrow and finish if you not doing anything."

"That's fine. Let me go to the bathroom, and we can go." It felt like my baby was tap dancing on my bladder, and I didn't think I was going to make it. But, when I sat down, and a large gush of fluid came out, I knew that wasn't pee.

"Shit, shit, shit," I cursed, then grabbed my phone from my purse so I could call my mama.

"Hey, baby."

"Please tell me you're at home." She didn't live far from here, so I knew she would make it to me in no time.

"No, I'm on my way downtown, why?"

"Shit, my water just broke."

"Vince, turn the car around, Ki's in labor! Where you at, baby?" she asked frantically.

"I'm in the bathroom at the clinic. I was just about to go home."

"Call the ambulance if you have to. I'll meet you at the hospital."

"OK." I hung up and texted Lo and Tae's parents to meet me at the hospital, too. Now I just had to figure out how I was going to get to the damn hospital.

I stood up and started feeling pressure, so I sat back down. I didn't know what that was going to do, but I hoped it kept this little boy in there a little longer.

Me: Can you come here for a second?

I texted Aaron, and he came knocking on the door seconds later. "Yeah?"

"Um... can you open the door, please?" The door slowly opened, and he stepped in with his hands over his eyes.

"You need some tissue or something?"

"No, I need you to go grab some towels, I think my baby is coming."

"WHAT?!" He dropped his hands, and his eyes were big as saucers. "W-what am I supposed to do?"

"Just get the towels and let's go. We can take my car if you don't want your seats to get wet, but I need to make it to the hospital, like now." Aaron backed up and ran into the wall, then turned to run out. This time when I stood up, I wiped and quickly pulled my sweatpants up. I wobbled out the bathroom and walked to the front door. Aaron was right behind me, and it looked like he had grabbed every towel he saw.

"I'm parked closer, come on." He opened the passenger door and threw the towels down any kind of way, then helped me in.

"I'm not going to make it to Trinity, just go to Christ," I instructed, and he pulled off from the curb with his tires screeching. We got caught at the light on 95th and Western, and by this time, my contractions were strong as hell, and they were literally a minute apart.

"I'm not gon' make it, I'm not gon' make it. It feels like he's coming out!" I screamed as I snatched my pants off. I reached down, and I felt the top of his head, and I knew for sure I wasn't going to make it to the hospital.

"Oh, hell naw, Kiarra, stop! Just wait, we almost there," Aaron panicked as I let my seat back and grabbed the extra towels from the back seat. "This girl about to have a baby in my front seat."

"Aaahh!" I screamed as I felt his head crowning.

"I'm finna throw up. I gotta throw up! Awk!" Aaron was whipping through traffic, and I was trying to focus on what was going on between my legs.

"Shut up and try not to kill us, please! Aaahhh," I screamed as another contraction ripped through my body. I gave one little push and felt instant relief as I reached down and pulled my son out. His little cries filled the car, and Aaron stared over at me in disbelief.

"Can you go inside and get help now?" I asked, laughing. He hopped out the car and ran inside the hospital. "Hey, little man, you just couldn't wait, huh?" I counted his ten tiny toes and little fingers and smiled at how perfect he looked. The passenger door opened, and there was a nurse there with a wheelchair and a heated blanket.

"Are you OK, ma'am?" My vision was blurred, and her voice sounded distorted. I knew then that something was wrong.

"Kiarra?" I heard Aaron call my name, but I couldn't respond.

"We need help out here!!" I heard someone yell as everything went black.

CHAPTER THIRTY-SEVEN
Lauren

"I'm looking for Kiarra Blak's room." When I got the text from Kiarra that she was having the baby, I was extra geeked, but when Aaron called and said something had happened and Ki passed out, I panicked, and we sped to the hospital.

"Here's your pass, she's in room 336," the lady at the front desk said, then pointed to the elevators. I took off with Adonis behind me and hopped on the elevator. The ride up to the third floor felt like it took years, and I wished I had taken the stairs instead.

"Bae, calm down," Adonis said, rubbing my shoulder as we stood in front of Ki's door. I took a deep breath, then opened the door.

"Look, Deontae, there go yo' godmommy." Kiarra was sitting up in the bed, holding the baby.

"Oh my God, I thought something happened to you. I almost had a heart attack," I said, wrapping my arms around her and the baby.

"My blood pressure just dropped, and that caused me to pass out, but we are both good."

"I'll give y'all some privacy. Congratulations, Ki," Adonis said.

"Thank you, and I think your brother is in the waiting room down the hall." Adonis nodded and left out the room. I washed my hands and got Baby Tae from her.

"Aaawww, Tator Tot, you look just like your sister

did, minus the eyes," I cooed.

"I know, right? I'm in love all over again."

"Me toooo. He is so cute, makes me have baby fever." Ki looked up at me, shocked, and I started laughing. "Don't you say nothing; my fever will go away the second I leave here." The door opened, and Tt Melissa came in with Vince behind her.

"Dang, I missed it again. Vince, I told you to drive faster," Tt Melissa said, pouting.

"He wasn't trying to wait on nobody. I had him in the front seat of Aaron's car," Ki said, laughing.

"Aw, hell naw, you'd be buying me a whole new car." I cringed thinking about it.

I stayed at the hospital until Deontae's parents came with Kenzie, and I left so they could spend some time with Ki and the baby, too. I walked into the waiting room to get Adonis, and Aaron looked pale.

"You good, bro?" I asked, laughing.

"Hell naw! After the shit I saw today, I will never be good again. I don't think I can even get in my truck again."

"I'm sure it wasn't that bad." Aaron looked at me crazy, and I laughed.

"She had a whole baby in my passenger seat. Like, it was towels and shit down, but that's not something you forget about."

Aaron's dramatic ass had his car towed to his house, and he rode with us back to the shop.

"When we gon' get started on our babies?" Adonis asked, wrapping his arms around me.

"The second my last name changes, I'll start thinking about babies. Until then, we won't be having anything, but we could have fun trying."

"Shiiiit, you ain't said nothing but a word. Come on."

"Boy, you better go get set up for yo' appointment," I waved him off and sat at the receptionist desk.

"A'ight, bet, I'll handle that later," Adonis said, walking off.

"Aye, Lo, do you have the keys to Kiarra's clinic?" Aaron asked, sitting across from me. "I want to go finish the job before she gets out the hospital."

"What time you tryna go? Now, before you answer, I don't get out my bed before eight o'clock unless I'm getting paid."

"A'ight, I can meet you there at nine then." He stood up and walked to the back, and I rolled my eyes. I should've told his ass before ten. I didn't see how people could get up early as hell on purpose. I was not one of those people, though.

***

Aaron

Man, after I watched Kiarra pull a whole-ass baby out of her shit, I had a newfound respect for women. The shit traumatized me for life, and I didn't think I could go through that a second time. Whenever it was time for me to have some kids of my own, I was going to have to sit outside or something. I damn sure wasn't having any more babies delivered in my ride.

I sent my truck to the shop to get detailed, but I

didn't think that would be enough for me not to cringe when I got in it.

"This is looking nice, Aaron!" Lauren said from behind me. I had just finished the mural Kiarra wanted, and I could honestly say this was my favorite piece I'd ever done.

"'Preciate it, sis." I took a few pictures on my phone and cleaned up my mess. Once I was done, Lauren locked up and set the alarm. "A'ight, Lo, I'll holla at you." I watched her pull off before I did the same.

I decided to take a ride around the city to clear my head, and before I knew it, I was parking at the hospital where Kiarra was. I still had her purse in my truck, so that was going to be my excuse in case I looked like a creep coming in there. After I made sure she was straight, I was going to go about my business.

After getting my visitor's pass from the front desk, I went to the gift shop to get some balloons and a bear for the baby. I took the elevator to the third floor and went to her room. The door was closed, so I knocked lightly and waited for her to tell me to come in.

"Come in!" I heard her yell, and I slowly opened the door. "Hey, what are you doing here?" she asked, sitting up in the bed with her eyebrows scrunched.

"I was coming to check on you and to give you your purse."

"Thank you, I appreciate you for making sure I got here safe, even if you were driving like a bat outta hell," she laughed.

"Look, I didn't know what was going on. I'm usually cool under pressure, but that was a whole different type of ball game there."

"If I wasn't in so much pain, I would've recorded you sitting there yelling louder than me, talking about you gotta throw up. I've never seen no grown man act like that before."

"Yeah, whatever, I ain't ashamed," I laughed. "But, let me get out yo' way. Congratulations, in case I didn't tell you already."

"Thank you." I left out the hospital and went home to shower and lay my ass back down. Guess I was having a lazy day today.

Chapter Thirty-Eight
Kiarra

After being cooped up in the hospital for two days, me and Little Tae were finally going home. I might be biased because they were mine, but I seriously think I have the most perfect babies ever. Deontae David Blak Jr. came into this world, eight pounds, nine ounces and twenty-two inches long. Just looking at the size of his feet and hands, I could tell he was definitely going to take after his father and grandfather with his size.

"Knock, knock. Hey, it's just me with the discharge papers for you and Baby," my nurse said, coming into the room. "Pretty simple instructions for you; no lifting anything heavier than the baby. Make sure you follow up with your doctor in four to six weeks, and no sex before then." I laughed when she said that part, because unless it was possible to have sex with a ghost, I had nothing to worry about.

"Make sure you follow up with your baby's pediatrician, and if he doesn't have one, there's a number here you can call. Dr. Hero is excellent with kids, and he's taking new patients. If you don't have any questions for me, sign both of these, and you're free to go." I signed the papers and waited for my mama to come back with the car seat. Once she did, I strapped Junior in securely, and we left out.

"Can you stop by the clinic before I go home?" I asked my mama from the back seat, and she smacked her lips.

"No. You tryna do some work, and you're fresh out the hospital?"

"I just want to see the mural I had done," I said with

my lip poked out.

"Ooohh, I saw it yesterday. It's the bomb, girl."

"Ma, you're showing yo' age. Nobody says 'bomb' anymore," I laughed.

"Whatever. Well, I'm bringing it back, shit." My mama drove to the clinic, and I told her I was just going to run in so I didn't have to take Junior out in the cold again.

When I went inside and looked at the mural, I was speechless, and I even shed a few tears. Yes, it was that good. Every section of the wall was a different representation of Chicago, and he had captured the best part of the city. Aaron had done his damn thing on this, for real, and I took a picture of it with my phone to get it blown up later.

I couldn't wait to get the doors open and to finally see my dream come to life. I know Deontae would've been proud to see how everything had come together. I took one final picture and left out so I could go home and enjoy my babies.

As I sat back and reflected on the last year of my life, I now understood that everything that had happened to me, the good and especially the bad, was preparing me for whatever God had planned for my future.

Epilogue

Kiarra

One year later…

Knock! Knock!

"Mommy?" I heard Kenzie's little voice from the other side of my door, so I got up and opened it.

"Good morning, babies, what's wrong?" Kenzie and DJ were standing there looking like they were up to no good.

"DJ boo-boo again, and I'm hungry," she said, holding her stomach. My daughter was such a drama queen, and I didn't know where she had gotten that from.

"OK, I'll change him, Kenzie, and you can go grab a banana. We're going out to eat with Papa and Nannie," I told her, referring to Deontae's parents. Her eyes lit up, and she clapped her hands.

"Yaaay! I'm going to put on my Shimmer and Shine, OK, mommy?" She took off running to her room, and I just shook my head.

"Come on, stinky man." I picked DJ up and went to his room to get him changed. Once he was all cleaned up, I got him dressed and went back to my room to do the same.

This past year had been anything but easy for me. Trying to juggle two kids and run a business had been a struggle, but I loved my babies, and I loved what I did, so it made it worth it at the end of the day. Besides, ever since my mom and Vince had moved back, they'd been a huge help with the kids. My mom even comes down to the clinic and works a few days a month when I decide to take a break, which isn't often.

"Mommy, I'm ready!" Kenzie popped up in my room, and she had her skirt on backward, and her shoes on the wrong foot.

"Good job, but let Mommy help you." After we were all dressed, we left out, and I drove to meet Mama Roxy and Dave at the cemetery. We tried to meet up a couple times a month, and I loved it because it made me feel closer to Tae. I was not quite ready to start dating again, but at least I didn't cry when I hear his name anymore.

This isn't the last you'll hear from me, though... AJ has some tricks up her sleeve.

As for everyone else, it's been great. Lauren is still crazy ol' Lauren. She and Adonis are still going hard, and he had been talking to me about proposing to her. I was happy my best friend had finally found someone who was all about her. I hadn't seen her this happy in a while.

Kodi and Gerald had got married last month and should be welcoming their first child any day now. I was so happy for them, Kodi especially. If there was anybody who needed a happy ending, it was Kodi. Kodi's career had taken off, and there were so many record companies trying to sign her, but she said she liked being independent.

Banks has been buried in his music, as always, but he stops by or calls a few times a week to check on us. I think he's still in denial about Lo moving on, but for the most part, he had stopped asking about her whenever we talked, so that was a step.

Well, that's the end for us... for now anyway!

The End!

A note from the Author

Thank you all for sticking with me through this journey with this crew. I know a lot of readers were upset with the way I ended part two, and I hope I made up for it with this finale. This isn't the last you'll hear from Kiarra; her story isn't over yet.

Go check out Shorty Fell In Love Again to see how Kiarra is handling life.

Connect with me!

Facebook: **A. Jovan** https://www.facebook.com/AuthorA.Jovan

Instagram: @ **a.jovan__** https://www.instagram.com/a.jovan__/

'LIKE' my author page **Authoress A. Jova'n** https://www.facebook.com/Authoress-A-Jovan-108036620541438/

Join my readers group: **A.Jova'n's Reading Haven** https://www.facebook.com/groups/1848207391862436/

Twitter: @**A_Jovan_**

Email: **authoressa.jovan@gmail.com**

YouTube: **AsToldByAJ** https://www.youtube.com/channel/UClJCTjWIzQ4Rn-adQ-pXOeA?view_as=subscriber

More great reads from A. Jova'n:

All of my previous books under 'AJ Dix' will be updated and released little by little. But, for now Enjoy these<3

Yedda & Swift: A Deranged Love Story 1 & 2

The Risks We Take For Love & Money 1 (collab w/DeeAnn)

Caught Up With A Chi-Town Hitta: A Forbidden Love 1 & 2

Pretty Girls Get Down With Hood Niggas 1

Made in the USA
Monee, IL
01 August 2021

74742209R00105